BENEATH THE CORSETS

We cannot force ourselves to love - or to withhold it. At best, we can curb our actions. The heart itself is beyond control. That is its power, and its weakness.

- CHITRA BANERJEE DIVAKARUNI

Love that we cannot have is the one that lasts the longest, hurts the deepest and feels the strongest.

- KAY KNUDSEN

There is a charm about the forbidden that makes it unspeakably desirable.

- MARK TWAIN

CHAPTER I

January 1905

Nina Monroe had always been a good wife to her husband, but she was sorry to say that her husband did not treat her with the same love and respect. The year was 1905 and London's industry was thriving thanks to the many factories, mills, and warehouses that loomed over the city, casting oppressive shadows over the narrow, cobbled streets, all the while infusing the air with clouds of smoke and dust. Nina's mind was similarly hazy, owing to the fact that she and her husband Lucas were once again required to attend one of *The Shrewd Seven*'s infamous drinking parties.

The Shrewd Seven had been an integral part of Nina's life ever since she could remember. Seven gentlemen friends (including Nina's father Edward Belmont) from seven wealthy and renowned families, had formed the society some forty-five years ago. To the outside observer, it functioned as a gentlemen's club, but in reality it was fundamentally clandestine and dishonest in nature. The men trafficked and sold opium (amongst other prohibited items) and used the profits to purchase the expensive alcohol and lavish furnishings that adorned the group's headquarters. There was no doubt in Nina's mind, either, that some of the proceeds went towards procuring prostitutes to entertain the men, which infuriated her deeply.

After the death of the seven founders, *The Shrewd Seven* was bequeathed to their sons and they were under strict instructions to withhold the tradition. Nina's father bore only three daughters, so he had no son to take his place. But Stefan Sinclair, Harry Sinclair, John Fawcett, Gareth Fawcett, Thomas Whittaker, Robert

Fitzgerald, Oscar Fitzgerald, James Monroe and Nina's husband Lucas Monroe now served under William Rosethorn (the leader), maintaining the society and funding their extravagant lifestyles by unlawful means. William Rosethorn's father, Henry, had been the leader of *The Shrewd Seven* during the first generation of members, and he had been a "murderous tyrant who became consumed by power" according to what Nina had overheard her father saying to her mother when she was a child. It appeared that William had inherited his father's dictatorial nature – he was a truly dangerous man, and sometimes Nina believed that the men only complied with his more treacherous demands out of fear, for she believed they were scared of what he might do to them and their wives and children.

For Nina, it was not a nice society to be affiliated with, and sometimes she cursed her father for bestowing this burden on her and her husband and son. However, she did not dare express these thoughts aloud to anyone, not even Lucas or her sisters. She did not like to think what might happen if anybody was to tell William that she felt this way.

The members of *The Shrewd Seven* were only permitted to marry within the seven founding families, lest too many people become aware of the society's secrets. So Lucas' and Nina's fathers, both members of the society, had agreed when their children were infants that they would marry and uphold their traditions and values. As a result of this, Nina often felt that she was not in control of her own life. Everything that she had become and everything that she was required to do had been decided for her by her father and the constraining rules and demands of *The Shrewd Seven*. Even her marriage was a miserable one – Lucas assured her that he loved her, but she knew that he had been having countless affairs for almost all of their nineteen years of marriage. Sometimes Nina fantasised about doing the same, but she knew that if Lucas ever found out, she would be cast out onto the street. Oh, the injustice of it all!

Similarly, the *Seven's* leader, William Rosethorn, seemed to have control over all of the people around him: the members of the group, the *wives* of the members (particularly Nina's eldest sister Lolita). He was even bribing London's chief police commissioner over a past misdemeanour involving sex with another man. It seemed that London, and all of the important people in it, were bent to William's will, and it seemed to all that he could bring anyone to their knees. Thus, Nina could see no way out of this life with The Shrewd Seven. It wasn't as though the police commissioner was about to let William reveal his secret to the authorities. Therefore, The Shrewd Seven would continue to operate for the foreseeable future, as far as Nina could see.

It was a cold winter night, and Nina's breath formed before her eyes as she, Lucas and their sixteen year-old son Daniel walked down the familiar marble pathway to Rosethorn Manor (the *Seven's* headquarters). After what seemed like an age, they arrived at the front door and were greeted by none other than William Rosethorn himself. His dark eyes glittered menacingly as he beheld his guests, and his dark hair shimmered in the moonlight. He was wearing a black suit with a black waistcoat which to Nina seemed to match the black heart that she knew resided in his cold chest.

"Ah! The Monroes have arrived! Welcome, do come in. Lucas, have a glass of scotch. Daniel, come and join the men for a drink. And Nina, the women are gossiping by the fire with some wine, I'm sure you would like to go and join them!"

Nina smiled a slightly sardonic smile but remained silent as William led them through the magnificent hallway with its glittering marble floor and grandiose marble staircase, and then through to the drawing room where the men were playing cards and drinking, and the women were indeed sat in armchairs by the fire. The room was lit only by gas lamps and the flickering light of the fire, which gave the room a slightly ominous aura. The portraits of the *Seven's* founding members on the scarlet walls seemed to watch Nina as she walked over to the women. To distract herself from this disconcerting thought, she made a mental note of all of the members that were present. There was: Nina's eldest sister Lolita and her husband Robert Fitzgerald; Robert's brother Oscar and his wife Elizabeth (who was Lucas' sister); Lucas' best friend Dr Stefan Sinclair; Stefan's brother Harry; Stefan's sister Georgina; his other sister Lyra with her husband Gareth Fawcett and daughter Anita (whom Daniel was currently courting); Gareth's brother John Fawcett and his sister Maria Fawcett; the Whittaker sisters Rosalyn and Lucy; and then of course Lucas, Daniel and the tyrannical William. Nina counted to herself. Yes, the Belmonts were here (her maiden name), the Monroes were certainly here, the Fitzgeralds, the Sinclairs, the Fawcetts, the Whittakers, the Rosethorn tyrant… The seven families were here but she still felt as though somebody was missing. She continued to look around as she suddenly realised that she could not locate her other older sister Evangeline and her husband Thomas Whittaker, nor their daughter Myrcella. Where were they?

As Nina drew closer to the women, her eldest sister Lolita caught her eye and beckoned to her to come and talk to her alone in a corner of the room, behind a room divider where the men could not see them. Lolita was starkly different from Nina. Whereas Nina had blonde hair, blue eyes, fair skin, and a humble and passive personality, Lolita had long, dark curly hair, dark eyes, wore lots of makeup, and was feisty and domineering. Lolita's eyes darted around the room and her chest heaved in her corset as she took a deep breath, clearly steeling herself for something.

"What's the matter, Lolita?" Nina asked.

"Nina, she's gone," Lolita whispered in a slightly frantic voice.

"Who is gone?" Nina asked, perplexed. She had never seen her sister looking so worried.

"Evangeline. Her and Thomas and Myrcella. They wrote a letter to me. They don't want to be a part of *The Shrewd Seven* any longer, so they have gone on the run."

Nina clapped a hand to her mouth.

"Oh god!" Nina exclaimed, knowing that William would not accept this. "Please tell me you haven't told William…"

Lolita blanched and started awkwardly.

"He needs to know, Nina…"

"But God knows what he will do to them if he ever finds them," Nina said darkly.

"I know that, but Eva said that is a risk she is willing to take. Besides, I can't keep this from him. He will find out eventually when they stop attending gatherings, and imagine what he will do to me if he finds out that I kept this from him…"

"I suppose," agreed Nina, "But aren't you his favourite? Perhaps you could try and convince him to let them go?"

Lolita was indeed William's favourite member of the *Seven*. She was the only woman that was permitted to work alongside the men in trafficking and selling. She was the only woman that was trained specifically by William. Nina often suspected that there was something more going on between the pair of them, but Lolita always denied it. Nina could see that Lolita's husband Robert Fitzgerald was growing suspicious too, but of course, he didn't dare to accuse their leader of sleeping with his wife. It wouldn't be worth the consequences if he did.

Lolita let out an incredulous laugh. "Don't be absurd! You know as well as I do what the price is for betrayal of the *Seven*."

Nina did know. How could Evangeline be so stupid? Stupid, or brave, she couldn't decide…

CHAPTER II

January 1905

As usual, the previous night's gathering at Rosethorn Manor had been tedious and uneventful for Nina. The men had overindulged on spirits and tobacco and had gambled away a fair portion of the *Seven*'s weekly takings. As Nina could have predicted, Lucas had spent the night talking and generally acting overfamiliar with a few of the women, namely his best friend Stefan's sister Georgina and of course, Rosalyn Whittaker. Oh yes, Rosalyn was a particular favourite of Lucas', with her ginger curls, full and heaving bodice, and heavily made up eyes and lips. Nina had watched, incensed, as the woman laughed at his jokes and caressed his arms all night. After a while, Nina had instead decided to observe the other men in the room. The most handsome of all of the men, had been of course Lucas' best friend Dr Stefan Sinclair. She had always admired him from afar, but in light of her husband's neglect of her, Stefan seemed to be even more attractive with his wavy dark hair, stubbly beard, prominent cheekbones and dark eyes. And of course, he was intelligent, being a doctor... No. Nina had had to distract herself with red wine to put a stop to such thoughts. Her attention had turned to her sister Lolita and the wretch William. He had been whispering in her ear and plying her with wine all night. From the way that Lolita gazed into his eyes, Nina could see that her sister was utterly devoted to and besotted with this hideous monster of a man. Why was William permitted to behave this way with his friend's wife? Why were any of the married men permitted to do as they pleased? She wondered when Lolita was going to tell William about her sister's departure... perhaps she had told him after the gathering. Perhaps he knew now and was plotting his next move...

Nina's reverie was suddenly disturbed by her husband stirring in the bed next to her. Lucas rolled over towards Nina, grunted and put his arms around her. To Nina's annoyance, he then began stroking her neck and kissing underneath her ears.

Nina gently lifted his arms away from her.

"Don't even think about touching me this morning, *darling*," she said, placing a sarcastic emphasis on the last word.

Lucas sighed and hoisted himself into a sitting position against the pillows. "What now, Nina?"

"You know exactly what now," she replied.

He rolled his eyes. "Do enlighten me."

Nina turned to look at him and raised her eyebrows. "You know perfectly well that I do not like it when you throw yourself at other women in front of me, as you were doing last night."

Lucas laughed. "I was hardly throwing myself at her, darling. It was definitely the other way around."

Nina threw him a withering look. "I won't even dignify that with a response," she said.

"Come now, Nina, you know that I love only you," Lucas said, still laughing.

It was Nina's turn to laugh, incredulously. "You love me? I don't think so! I don't think you understand what loving somebody means, Lucas. Tell me, is she your latest mistress then? If she is, then I don't want you anywhere near me – God knows where she has been!"

"As a matter of fact," Lucas snarled, "She *is* my mistress. And what business is it of yours?"

Nina was stung. "I am your wife, Lucas, and you should treat me with respect."

It was futile. How many times had they had this same argument?

"Nina, I do respect you. There are things –" He began, but Nina interrupted him.

"*Things a husband cannot do with his wife*, I know, Lucas, I know that is your twisted belief. I have heard it a thousand times. Or perhaps it is your way of convincing yourself that you are still a good husband to me. How would you feel if I started having affairs with other men?"

Lucas sneered. "You wouldn't. You can't. You are my wife, and that is the end of it."

"I can't!" Nina repeated hysterically. Just as she was about to continue, Lucas seized one of her wrists with a tight grip. When he spoke, his voice was dangerously quiet.

"I said that is the end of it, Nina."

And with that, he swept out of bed and out of the room. Nina was furious. She did not want to give him the satisfaction of crying over him, but of course, her eyes betrayed her and she began to sob against the pillows.

After a few moments her heart jolted as she heard the bedroom door open, and she was just about to cease sobbing and wipe her eyes when she realised that it wasn't Lucas, but her servant Lottie, with a tray full of breakfast. Lottie was a young girl, not much older than Nina's son Daniel, and she and Nina had quite a close bond. Well, as close as a mistress can have with a servant, anyway.

"Mistress Nina! What is the matter? Has the Master upset you again?"

Lottie sat on the bed and patted Nina's arm.

"No, Lottie, I am alright," she lied.

"I brought you some breakfast, Mistress," she said. "Once you have finished I will help you to dress for the day ahead. Master Lucas says that Mr Rosethorn will be visiting the manor in a couple of hours."

Fantastic, thought Nina. Just what she needed.

CHAPTER III

January 1905

All of the grandfather clocks in Monroe Manor struck one simultaneously, chiming ominously through the many hallways. Right on cue, the doorbell downstairs rang too, which added to the cacophony of chimes. Nina sighed and resigned herself to the fact that she would have to greet and spend time with William and possibly some of his cronies from the *Seven*. Just as she was about to leave the master bedroom, Lucas flung the door open.

"He's here, Nina!" he barked.

"I know, I'm not deaf," she said through gritted teeth.

She noticed that Lucas did not wait for her. He had raced ahead, presumably to fetch Daniel from his quarters.

As Nina walked down the grand marble staircase to the entrance hall, she tried to push all of her negative thoughts out of her mind. Their butler Christopher Harper had opened the doors to reveal William Rosethorn, wearing a dark suit and a frown, and also Dr Stefan Sinclair.

"Mr Rosethorn and Dr Sinclair, Mistress Nina," said Harper, beckoning the men to cross the threshold.

Nina walked forwards to greet them and to her horror, William took her hand in his own and raised it to his lips.

"My dear Nina, where are Lucas and Daniel?" he said when he released her.

"On their way down, Mr Rosethorn," she said, trying not to wince as his whiskery beard scratched her knuckles.

As Nina moved to greet Stefan, she found herself holding her breath as her eyes met his. There was a slight pause and then Stefan too raised her hand to his lips, which made her heart flutter.

"Nina, how lovely to see you," he said, smiling. His dark eyes twinkled and his cheek bones became even more prominent. Inwardly, Nina hoped that her eyes were not too swollen from crying earlier that morning, and she also scolded herself for not having had the foresight to apply any makeup. She looked down to see that he was wearing a crisp white shirt and dark waistcoat, but the neck of his shirt was unbuttoned, revealing some of his chest. Nina found herself wondering what he would look like were more of it unbuttoned...

"Ah, Lucas, Daniel, there you are," said William pompously (as though they were some of his servants.) "Let us go to the drawing room, shall we? Harper, some ale perhaps? And a red wine for the lady?"

Nina could not believe that he was leading the way and giving orders to the servants in a house that was not even his own. How arrogant of him. Nevertheless, they walked in silence to the drawing room. Nina linked arms with her son Daniel and noted how anxious he seemed to look. He was very like Lucas – short blonde hair, penetrating grey eyes and a clean shaven face. But at the moment, his hands were shaking and he was biting his bottom lip. Despite his age, Nina still thought of him as her little boy, and she loved him with all of her heart. It pained her to think that he might be worrying about something.

"Are you okay, Danny?" she whispered.

"Yes, I'm fine, mother," he replied, looking straight ahead.

And so they all took their seats in the drawing room, which, though magnificent, was still not as grandiose as the one in Rosethorn Manor. The walls were dark green and the floor was made of dark wood. Many bookcases filled with books adorned the walls. Light streamed in from the open windows, but Nina couldn't help but feel that she was imprisoned in her own drawing room. William took a seat directly in front of the hearth and beckoned for the others to sit in a semi-circle around him: Lucas on his left, Stefan on his right, Daniel next to Lucas and Nina next to Stefan. Harper brought a tray filled with drinks for them all. The men sipped their ale while Nina proceeded to drain her glass of wine in one. Lucas reproached her disdainfully with his eyes while they waited for William to speak.

"Friends, today is a very special day. Before I told the rest of *The Shrewd Seven*, I wanted to make an announcement to you directly," William began.

Nina's stomach jolted. In her experience, William's announcements were not usually good news – for her, at least.

"Or rather," he said slowly, "Daniel would like to make an announcement. Isn't that right, Danny?"

Nina flinched as William called her son by her pet name for him. She watched, aghast, as her sixteen-year-old son stood to address their small group.

"I have decided that I would like to do some volunteer work at the hospital with you, Stefan," Daniel said, looking at Stefan, who beamed back at him.

"Oh, wonderful, Danny!" cried Nina, relieved. She knew that her son had always had a keen interest in becoming a doctor, so she was thrilled. "You will make a fantastic doctor someday, won't he, Stefan?"

Lucas clapped Daniel on the back and Stefan nodded in agreement.

"Absolutely. I will do everything in my power to see that you are well looked after," he said. "You can start this week, I will arrange it all."

Nina gazed longingly at Stefan. He was so kind and thoughtful. Why couldn't Lucas be like him?

"Oh thank you, Stefan," She said, "This is wonderful news,

Danny."

Just as Nina's heart began to soar with happiness, it became punctured as William's next words registered with her.

"And the other news, Daniel. Tell them the other news." William said eagerly.

"Oh, yes," Daniel started, and he began to bite his lip again.

"I have decided," he said (though Nina suspected that that was not true as his eyes were fixed on William), "that I am now ready to commence work with *The Shrewd Seven*,"

If Nina's stomach had jolted before, it was nothing compared to what it was doing now.

Her baby boy was to join *The Shrewd Seven?* She could not bear the thought of him trafficking drugs and stealing and doing whatever else they did in the *Seven*. No, he was supposed to become a doctor... Her thoughts raced so much that they began to make her dizzy. She was hardly aware of the men cheering and hugging each other. No, all she could do was keep silent and hope that her narrowing peripheral vision wouldn't cause her to faint...

And suddenly, everything went black.

CHAPTER IV

January 1905

Hushed voices. Musky perfume. A sliver of sunlight through the drapes. Nina began to stir, and she became vaguely aware of two figures standing close to her.

"What is wrong with her, then?"

"Shock, I think,"

Nina's eyes snapped open. Perhaps it had been a dream.

"Nina!" cried Lolita. Her dark curls were askew, as though she had combed her fingers through them many times, and her eyes were bloodshot with worry. "Are you alright?"

Nina raised herself into a seated position. She was on one of the sofas in the drawing room, and somebody had placed a blanket over her.

"Yes, I am fine," she said. "What happened?"

Nina jumped as Stefan answered from behind her. "We were sitting here in the drawing room and Daniel told you of his plans to join *The Shrewd Seven*, and then, you... you lost consciousness."

Her stomach plummeted. So it hadn't been a dream.

"How long have I been lying here?" she asked.

"Fifteen minutes or so. Lolita arrived right after you... fainted," Stefan said. Nina felt the colour rising in her cheeks. "Lucas, Daniel and William have left for Rosethorn Manor as they are meeting with the rest of the *Seven* to make the announcement. William said that Lolita and I could stay here to care for you. Now that you are awake, I must go and join them. Please don't overexert yourself. Stay lying down, and Lolita will attend to you."

"So it's true then. He's really doing it?" Nina asked. Her voice was shaky with emotion.

Stefan gazed at her for a moment. His expression was unreadable.

"Yes, he's really doing it," he said quietly, running his hand through his smooth, dark hair. "Take care, Nina."

He stooped, lifted her limp hand in his, and placed it to his lips. The sensation of his lips on her skin was electrifying. Nina took care to conceal any outward display of emotion, as Lolita was of course watching.

As he left, Lolita closed the huge oak door behind him.

"Nina, you ought to be careful," Lolita said.

"Sorry?"

"William was suspicious of your fainting," she continued. "He suspected that you fainted because you didn't want Daniel to join the *Seven*, but I assured him that you were merely overcome because your son was growing up too fast,"

"He is just a boy," Nina said quietly, "I don't want him to do all the things you have done, to see all the things that you have seen…" Images of guns, knives, and crates of drugs and money flashed through Nina's mind. She began massaging her temples as though she were trying to erase the thoughts.

"Daniel is nearly seventeen," Lolita said sternly. "He is a man, Nina. He should be honoured to join the *Seven*. And *you* should feel honoured that your son will be the youngest ever to join. William obviously thinks that he is capable. He must show great potential."

Nina's voice became slightly higher in volume and pitch.

"Daniel is simply too young to be a part of that world. You don't have any children. You don't understand…"

Lolita opened her mouth to retort but surreptitiously placed her hand over her stomach for a split second. This did not go unnoticed by Nina, who frowned.

"If I had a child," Lolita said in a voice barely more than a whisper, "I would gladly offer them up for service in the *Seven*."

Her words hung around them in the air for a few uncomfortable moments.

"You need to be careful, Nina, that your actions cannot be interpreted as disloyalty to the *Seven*, because as you know, William does not tolerate disloyalty." Lolita continued.

"I am not disloyal," Nina said angrily, "I am just a mother who is worried about her son!"

"Alright," Lolita said, and sat down beside Nina on the sofa. "There is something else I need to talk to you about. I am sure that William would have told the rest of the *Seven* by now, anyway so I am sure he will not mind me telling you now."

"What is it? What else could it possibly be?" Nina said wearily.

"I told him about Evangeline. I showed him the letter, and Nina, he is not happy." Lolita said, her eyes brimming with tears. She was clearly torn between her loyalty to William and the *Seven* and her love for their sister.

"Oh," said Nina. "What did he say?"

Lolita took a few breaths to steady herself. "He says that he is going to find them, and kill them,"

The two sisters stared at each other for a few agonising moments. There was no doubt in Nina's mind that William would indeed do as he said. She put her hands over her eyes and leaned on her older sister's shoulder, unsure of what to say next. She did not dare to curse William in front of Lolita, who clearly adored him.

"They knew what it would mean for them when they decided to leave," Lolita said, brushing away her tears. "So they have only got themselves to blame, really."

Nina made a noise of agreement, which was muffled by the material of her sister's dress. The two sisters sat together in comfortable silence until Nina fell asleep again. All of this *Shrewd Seven* business was simply draining.

*

"Nina, wake up," said the harsh voice of her husband, later that evening.

Nina opened her eyes. The oil lamps were now lit and the sky outside was dark. She must have slept all afternoon. There was no sign of Lolita. She sat up again, pushing the blanket away.

"How are you feeling, darling?" Lucas said. "I have been worried about you."

"I am fine," Nina said. "Where is Daniel?"

"He is upstairs," Lucas said, pulling Nina close to him. "Please don't worry about him joining the *Seven*, darling. He was very mature during our meeting this afternoon. I think he will be a fantastic addition to the group."

Nina's mind was still heavy with the disturbing images of guns and knives.

"But he is just a boy," she said weakly.

"He is a man, darling," Lucas said, putting his arms around her and stroking her hair.

Nina breathed in the scent of the skin on his neck and was horrified to discover that he smelled strongly of women's perfume. It wasn't hers.

She wriggled out of Lucas' embrace.

"Where have you been?" Nina asked accusingly.

"What do you mean? I have been at Rosethorn Manor at the meeting..." Lucas said.

"After that," she snapped. "Where were you after that? Don't lie to me."

Lucas sighed.

"Alright, I was with Rosalyn. But I don't think that it is any of your business…"

"Of course it is my business!" she cried. "Oh, you were *so* worried about me today weren't you? Worried enough to leave me after I fainted. Worried enough to go and spend some time with another woman on your way home."

"Nina…" Lucas started, but she swept out of the room like a whirlwind and strode through the hallway of Monroe Manor, stopping only to retrieve her coat from the coat stand, and to retrieve a bottle of wine from one of the sideboards. Harper was standing by the front door.

"Where are you going, Mistress Nina?"

"Anywhere but here," she said sternly and ordered Harper to open the door. She stepped out into the night, relieved that her husband wasn't following her.

As the stones crunched beneath her boots, she decided that there was only one person who would understand her feelings at this moment…

CHAPTER V

January 1905

Nina swayed unsteadily as she knocked on the oak wooden door in front of her. The light emanating from the oil lamp next to the door irritated her tired eyes, and she winced as she caught sight of her reflection in one of the door's glass panes. Her blonde hair was wavy and had been swept this way and that by the wind on her journey. Her blue eyes were unfocused and she was sure that she had acquired more lines at their outer corners. Nina did not have time to dwell on these imperfections, however, as the door swung open to reveal Dr Stefan Sinclair, wearing a burgundy dressing gown and a bemused frown.

"Nina!" he cried. "To what do I owe the pleasure at this late hour?"

"I wanted to see you," Nina said breathlessly, blushing at the sight of him in his night time attire. She also realised that this was probably the first time that they had ever been alone together. Stefan had been in their lives for years, but any time he and Nina were at the same event, there were always other people around. Not this time.

His brown, round eyes studied Nina's forlorn features and then rested on the empty bottle of wine that she was still clutching in her left hand.

"Ah," he said with a knowing, sympathetic smile. He welcomed her inside and took her coat from her.

"Please come in and sit down," he said, leading her into his drawing room. "I would offer you a glass of wine, but I can see that you have already had some."

Nina cursed herself as she took a seat in a winged armchair. She had not meant to drink the entire bottle, but somehow she had lost track of how much she had been consuming.

Stefan pushed a glass of water into her shaking hands and then took a seat in the chair opposite her.

"Tell me," he said thoughtfully, tracing his lips with his finger, "Why have you come here tonight, Nina? Does Lucas know you are here?"

She took a sip from her glass and when she looked at him again, he was gazing at her with an expression of mingled curiosity and concern.

She took a deep breath.

"A million reasons, and no, he does not. We had an argument and I left the manor," she said quietly, trying not to cry and pour out all of her feelings at once.

"I see," Stefan said, running a hand through his dark hair. "Are you alright? Is there anything I can do to help you?"

Nina's expression softened even more. He seemed to genuinely care about her and her feelings.

"Lucas does not understand why I am worried about Daniel joining the *Shrewd Seven*," Nina began. "He says that Daniel is a man and that he will do well, but I am so scared, Stefan. He is just a boy. I don't think he is mature enough to deal with all of that responsibility. I would do anything to shelter him from that life, even for a few more years. Do you understand, Stefan? Please say that you understand..."

"I do understand. I understand a great deal," he said quietly, but he did not elaborate.

"Would you speak to William? Would you persuade him that Daniel is too young, too innocent to partake in the *Seven's* activities?" Nina begged. "There is no point in asking Lucas - he would not. But you are one of William's most trusted allies and one of his closest friends. Please... could you speak to him? Perhaps you could make him understand?"

Stefan leaned forwards and took both of her hands in his.

"Once William has made up his mind about something, there is no changing it, I am afraid," he said. "If I tried to persuade him to decide otherwise, it would only strengthen his resolve."

Nina was afraid of that.

"What if my poor little boy makes a mistake on a job and gets caught and sent to prison?" she whimpered, tears falling from her tired eyes.

Stefan stood up and moved towards her. He knelt at the side of her armchair and wiped her tears with a handkerchief.

"Listen Nina, I cannot persuade William to change his mind, but… it might be possible for me to… help Daniel," Stefan said.

Nina's eyes widened. "Oh, Stefan! Would you? Would you look out for him? Will you see that he comes to no harm? Please…"

There was a pause as they gazed into each other's eyes.

"I will," Stefan said, at last.

"Thank you," Nina said, taking hold of one of Stefan's hands and pressing her lips to it. "You are a good man, Stefan."

Stefan smiled at her, but it was a pained smile, as though he were having an inward battle with himself.

"Come now, Nina, it is late. Allow me to get dressed and I will walk home with you."

Nina shuddered. "No! I cannot go back home tonight, Stefan. Lucas does not like it when I drink, and heaven knows what he will think if he sees that I have been with you…" She blushed at the thought.

"I see," Stefan said. Nina couldn't help but notice that there was a distinct twinkle in his eye that was not there before. "Then I can provide accommodation for you tonight. I will ask the servants to set up one of the guest rooms. Excuse me…"

He quitted the room and Nina let out a deep sigh. Being so close in proximity to Stefan was agonising for her. He was handsome, kind and thoughtful. More kind and thoughtful than Lucas had been lately. Was she a bad person for thinking so tenderly of her husband's best friend? Just as she began to contemplate this at greater depth, Stefan appeared once again in the doorway.

"Your room is ready, Nina," he said. "Allow me to show you the way,"

As she was unsteady on her feet, Stefan took her arm in his and helped her to climb the stairs.

"Do you think me tiresome, Stefan?" Nina asked as they walked.

He turned to look at her. "Now, why would you ask such a thing?" he said incredulously.

"I know that you know that Lucas has had many mistresses and affairs during our marriage," she said. "It has been bothering me lately. I think I must be tiresome, or unattractive, or both."

Stefan shifted uncomfortably. After a slight pause he spoke. "You are neither of those things, Nina. I can assure you."

"Then why is he unfaithful to me?" Nina asked.

"I really don't know, Nina. Besides, I don't really want to get involved in your marital affairs."

Nina thought this was ironic, considering they were currently alone together at his home, and he was leading her upstairs to bed.

"Lucas is my best friend, but I do not pretend to understand the way a husband's mind works. All I know is that if you were my wife, I do not think that I would be unfaithful to you. I don't know why he is, Nina, I really don't."

Nina was silent and her heart soared with longing. *If you were my wife...*

All too soon, they came to a halt in front of a wooden door with a brass handle.

"Here is your room." Stefan said. "Have a good night's sleep and I will send one of the servants to wake you in the morning so you can walk home. Unfortunately, I am working early at the hospital so I will not see you in the morning."

Stefan took hold of her shoulders and kissed her cheek. His beard grazed against her skin and she found herself closing her eyes and putting her hand on the side of his neck. As he withdrew from kissing her cheek, they gazed at each other eagerly. Nina could feel heat rising in her face, and her heart skipped jubilantly as Stefan's face moved towards hers. His lips crushed against hers and he placed his arms around her waist. She kissed him back passionately and ran her hands through his dark, sleek hair. After a few moments, he pulled away from her. He was flustered and breathless.

"I'm sorry, Nina. Forgive me…"

"Don't be sorry, Stefan…" she said feverishly.

"No. I should not have done that." He said, shaking his head. "You are upset. You have argued with Lucas. You are worried about your son. You have been drinking. I am sorry. Good night, Nina."

He made to walk away but Nina called after him.

"Stefan, come back…"

"No, I mustn't," he said. "You are my best friend's wife. I want to, Nina. I really do. But I mustn't. Please forget that this happened. Good night."

He walked away down the dark hallway and Nina stepped into the guest room and closed the door behind her. She leaned against the closed door with her hand over her heart, her mind still reeling with the memory of the kiss and the smell of Stefan's skin so close to hers…

Forget that he kissed her? She could as easily detach one of her legs…

CHAPTER VI

January 1905

The next morning, Nina left Sinclair Manor with a plan. She would creep quietly to one of the guest rooms at home, change into her nightwear and emerge from the room pretending that she had been at home all night. However, as Nina crossed the threshold of Monroe Manor, Lucas was sitting on one of the settees in the hallway, drinking brandy and staring at her coldly. Her heart began beating wildly against her chest.

"And where have you been all night?" Lucas asked, in a voice that told her that he was less than impressed.

"Out," she replied and made to walk past him and ascend the grand staircase.

As she passed, he stood up and took hold of her arm.

"I can see that you were out," he said through gritted teeth. "I am asking you where you have been, and you *will* give me a straight answer," he said dangerously.

"I... I..." she started, wishing that she had had the sense to devise a convincing lie beforehand. "I don't know..."

"You don't know?" he said, turning her roughly to look at him.

"I was just walking," she said. "Just walking..."

But for Lucas, the terror behind her eyes was as good as a confession.

"Just walking!" he repeated sardonically. "You return here in last night's clothing... I can smell wine on your breath... Have you been with a man?"

He took hold of her shoulders and he was becoming so angry

that his grip on her was beginning to hurt.

"Lucas, you are hurting me," she said weakly.

"Have you been with a man?" he cried again.

"I... I..." she said, her mind practically whirring as she attempted to concoct a story.

Nina was unaware of the front door opening behind them. All she heard was a woman's voice shouting and suddenly Lucas' grip on her slackened. Nina closed her eyes with relief, and when she opened them, she saw her sister Lolita gripping Lucas' arm and her face was inches from his. Her eyes were glittering dangerously and she was shaking with fury. She had obviously pulled Lucas away.

"Don't ever touch my sister like that again," she said in a voice so chilling that Lucas seemed to recoil for a moment.

"Nina was with me last night," Lolita continued. "So you can stop with the accusations."

Nina sighed. Why didn't she think of that? She suddenly felt a rush of gratitude towards her older sister. Lolita had always looked out for her, ever since they were children.

"Ha!" Lucas laughed, his eyes popping furiously. "As if I'm going to believe that. This is just one whore covering for another!"

Lolita slapped him squarely across the face, leaving an angry red welt on his cheek.

"I don't care what you think of me, but how dare you insinuate that my sister – your wife – is a whore. You don't deserve her."

"If it weren't for your current predicament, Lolita, I would wipe the arrogant smirk from your face," Lucas growled.

Lolita stared, nonplussed, for a moment. "I would like to see you try," she said angrily. "Come on, Nina, let's go upstairs."

And with that, she took hold of Nina's hand and the two sisters climbed the stairs.

"I hope you were with a man," Lolita whispered as they walked. "It is no less than that bastard deserves."

Nina did not know how to respond to this. Her head was pounding.

"Thanks for pulling him away from me," she said at last.

Lolita was so strong and fearless. Nina often thought that she was stronger than some of the men. She envied her.

"No problem," Lolita said. "As I told you and mother when father died, I would always look out for you..."

*

Half an hour later, the two sisters were sitting at the dressing table in the master bedroom styling their hair and applying their makeup.

"What did Lucas mean when he said 'your current predicament', Lolita?" asked Nina as she powdered her nose.

"Oh. Yes. That." Lolita said. "That is what I came here to talk to you about." She took a deep breath and started to unfasten the corset of her dress.

"Erm...what are you doing?" asked Nina, confused.

"Just bear with me," Lolita said impatiently. At last, Lolita removed her dress and stood before Nina wearing only a satin slip which clung to her body. Nina could see that now, once Lolita's dress - with its many skirts and layers - was removed, Lolita's stomach was protruding more than normal. Yes, there was definitely a bump there.

"Lolita!" Nina gasped excitedly. "You are pregnant!"

"Yes. Around four months along. I can't hide it any longer," Lolita explained. "The men in the *Seven* know. After you fell asleep yesterday, I went to the meeting and told them. William made them swear that they wouldn't say a word to anyone because he thinks that it might make me vulnerable to our enemies."

"But Lolita, this is nothing to hide, this is wonderful!" said Nina and hugged her sister.

"Nina, you know as well as I that I don't have a maternal bone in my body," Lolita said blankly.

"Oh, but you will, Lolita!" Nina cried. "You will make an excellent mother. Is Robert happy?"

Lolita smirked. "Robert? I would be very surprised if it were his, considering he and I have not slept together in months and months."

"Oh," Nina said. Nina knew that her sister slept with plenty of other men besides her husband, and she suspected that she might even be sleeping with William. But Lolita not sleeping with her husband came as a shock to Nina.

"Then who is the father?" she continued.

Lolita shrugged. "I'm not sure. There are a few possibilities..." she said vaguely, but Nina noticed that Lolita seemed unable to look her in the eye.

"Robert has left me," Lolita continued. "Not that I care much. And not that it will make much difference. We will still be attending the *Seven* meetings together and technically, Robert and I can't legally divorce as William says it would disrupt the *Shrewd Seven*. But still..."

Nina gasped. "Oh, Lolita, I am so sorry!"

"Don't be," Lolita said, waving her hand dismissively. "I have plenty of other men that adore me. And besides, they are better than him."

Nina hugged her sister again, wondering what on earth their mother would say about this were she alive. When they broke apart, Lolita regarded Nina very seriously and she started to put her dress on again.

"So now for a word of caution, Nina. If you were with a man last night, then I am delighted for you, but please be careful. You don't want to end up in this… predicament."

"I…" started Nina.

"It's alright, Nina, I will find out eventually," said Lolita with a smirk. "Feel free to use me as an alibi anytime you need to. But just be careful."

Lolita walked back to the dressing table and applied some rouge lipstick.

"There, I am ready," she said. "Are you? We mustn't keep William waiting. The men will be waiting for the next meeting at Rosethorn Manor now."

Nina's heart skipped a beat. Of course. Caught up in all of her own drama, she had forgotten about today's meeting. She glanced at her reflection in the mirror. Her hair was curled and put up into an elegant up-do, and her makeup was flawless.

Despite her sister's warning, Nina could not help but feel elated. After his hospital shift, Stefan would attend the meeting, and this time, when he saw her, she would be looking her best. She jumped up from her seat and followed her sister out of the room.

CHAPTER VII

January 1905

If the drawing room at Rosethorn Manor was extravagant, it was nothing compared to the dining room. A magnificent, glittering chandelier hung from the high ceiling, bathing the room in its rich, sparkling light. The panelled walls were emerald in colour and were adorned with many prestigious paintings of landscapes and ancient battles. A colossal, rectangular, oak dining table was assembled in the centre of the room with eighteen, high-backed wooden chairs around its edges.

As Nina and Lolita walked into the room, arm in arm, Nina could see that most of *the Shrewd Seven* had already arrived, and had already taken their seats. William was seated at the head of the table. Lucas was on his left, and there were two empty chairs on his right, obviously reserved for Stefan and Lolita. So, Stefan had not arrived yet. Nina closed her eyes as she felt the familiar pang of longing in the pit of her stomach. Her eyes continued to rove around the room, taking in her surroundings.

"Oh my god, the little troll," Lolita hissed suddenly in her ear.

"What?" Nina whispered.

"Look at her, sitting there beside Lucas as bold as brass. I won't have it," Lolita said, breathing heavily.

Nina focused on Lucas again, and to her absolute horror, she noticed that Rosalyn Whittaker was sitting in the seat between Lucas and Daniel – *her* seat. Nina felt a twinge of anger deep within, but she patted her sister gently on the arm.

"Don't rise, Lolita," she warned. "I don't really care. I will just sit with you."

"No, I'll tell her, I'll…" Lolita started. She could see that her elder sister was becoming enraged on her behalf.

"Calm down, sister. I don't –"

Before Nina could finish her sentence, however, Lolita had marched off in the direction of Lucas' brazen mistress.

"Get out of my sister's seat now," Lolita commanded.

Rosalyn turned and looked down her heavily made up nose at Lolita. "I wasn't aware that Madame Monroe would be joining us for the meeting. She didn't come last time."

"So you thought you would take her place today, did you? Not on my watch. Move!"

"Really, Lolita, Lucas and I were in the middle of a conversation –" Rosalyn began, blinking rapidly.

"I don't care what you were in the middle of," Lolita snapped. Her eyes flashed dangerously and her dark curls seemed to stand on end. "My sister is Lucas' wife and she will sit beside her husband and son. You are nothing. You can't fuck your way into the inner circle of the *Seven*. Now, move."

Rosalyn raised her eyebrows at Lolita's language. "I beg your pardon," she simpered, "It seems to have worked perfectly for you, hasn't it?"

Lolita took a deep, rattling breath and clenched her fists so tightly that Nina was sure that she heard her knuckles crack.

William, who had been observing this altercation with mingled exasperation and amusement, stood up at last.

"Now, now, ladies," he said with a smirk. "Please, let's have none of this at the dining table. Rosalyn, kindly take your usual seat further down, and Lolita, come and sit down."

The sound of William's voice seemed to subdue the worst of Lolita's anger. She swept to her seat and sat down in silence, but continued to glower at Rosalyn as she too, took her seat. With an air of triumph, Nina sat down between her husband and son.

She looked straight ahead of her as Lucas placed his hand on her knee.

William snapped his fingers, and just like that, the servants of Rosethorn Manor emerged from the edges of the room and started to serve luncheon. It didn't take long for the large dining table to become laden with dishes and trays. Nina had to admit, William certainly did know how to cater for his guests. There were trays of roast chicken and turkey, dishes brimming with every vegetable imaginable, and mounds of potatoes of every variety. The servants circled the table, filling everybody's plate with delicious food. The guests started to eat and engage in idle chit-chat. Nina, however, only spoke to her son. He was to commence his volunteer work at the hospital the following day, and he seemed to be eager to start, which pleased Nina. Lucas attempted to engage Nina in conversation several times, but she ignored him and continued to eat. Nina noticed how Lolita leaned over Stefan's empty chair to speak to William, emphasising her heaving chest. Lolita hung on William's every word and William had a mischievous twinkle in his eye that told Nina that their conversation was probably not one that was appropriate for the dining table. Nina glanced at Robert, Lolita's husband, who, despite his insistence that they were separated, was still required to take his place beside his estranged wife. He looked less than impressed at his wife's open flirtation with their leader, but what could he say?

An hour passed, and as the servants finished collecting the last of the dishes, the dining room door opened, and in walked Stefan, wearing a dark suit, waistcoat and tie. His dark hair was windswept from his journey, and Nina noticed that he looked tired and slightly stressed.

"Please excuse my tardiness, William," Stefan said. "There was a delay with a patient." Stefan's eyes swept around the room and for a split second, his gaze fell upon Nina. He quickly looked away.

"No problem, my friend," said William. "Good God, man, you look exhausted. Come in and sit down," He pulled out Stefan's chair for him.

"I know. I'm afraid I did not sleep much last night," He paused and his eyes flashed towards Nina's general vicinity. "And then of course, the patients have been very demanding this morning,"

"How rude of them, being ill and decrepit in a hospital," laughed William. "I'm afraid you have missed luncheon but the main meeting is about to begin. Stefan, would you care to take notes?"

Stefan removed his jacket and hung it on the back of his seat. Nina noticed how the muscles on his arms protruded through the material of his shirt. *Stop it*, she told herself. She watched as Stefan reached into his bag and took out some parchment, ink, and a pen, and began to write the date at the top of the parchment.

"Well, now that we are all fed and watered," William began, addressing the room. Everybody fell silent and looked at him. "I would just like to remind everybody of Lolita's current condition. She is with child, and I cannot stress how important it is that we keep this knowledge to ourselves. If the peelers found out about this, then I'm sure that they would use this to their advantage."

The members nodded in agreement and Lolita scowled to herself. Nina noticed that Robert shifted uncomfortably in his seat.

"Also, I am pleased to say that Daniel will commence his formal training with myself this week,"

The members offered their congratulations whereas Nina remained silent.

"Furthermore," William continued, "I am sure you will be glad to know that my eyes and ears are working overtime trying to locate the traitor Thomas Whittaker and his wife and daughter. There are no new leads, but I am confident that we will find them in due course."

William's 'eyes and ears' referred to the many men around London that William paid in exchange for information. Nina closed her eyes, wishing that she were anywhere but here.

"And, most extraordinarily, the men at the Millwall Docks have informed me that they are expecting a rather large shipment of artillery weapons in three days' time. It would be a *crying shame* if one of the crates just happened to go missing, wouldn't it?" William sneered.

The men cheered in jubilant agreement. Nina tried hard to conceal her exasperation.

"William, I would like to volunteer myself for this assignment," Lolita said eagerly as the cacophony of cheers began to die down. Once again, she leaned over the table towards William, as though mere words could not demonstrate her longing for closeness.

"I appreciate that, Lolita," William said, looking deeply into her eyes. "Anybody else?"

"William, can Daniel and I possibly be excused from this? We will be working late at the hospital on that particular night," Stefan asked.

Nina became frozen with silent gratitude. A rush of emotions soared around her body but she didn't dare to open her mouth lest anybody would become suspicious. She waited for William's response with bated breath.

"Of course, Stefan and Daniel, you can be excused," William said at last.

Nina closed her eyes with relief, but her relief was short-lived as Lucas' voice permeated her consciousness.

"William, if I may, might I suggest that I take the lead on the assignment, due to Lolita's… condition? She can accompany me, by all means, but I think it would be better if I managed it?"

William considered this for a moment. Lolita opened her mouth in outrage but William held his hand out in order to pacify her obvious indignation.

"I think that would be for the best," William said coolly. "Alright, so Lucas will lead and Lolita will join him. Any other takers?"

There were a few murmurs of assent from the other men around the table.

"Excellent!" said William. "I would be most obliged if the people not partaking in this assignment could take their leave now, while we discuss the formalities. The meeting is adjourned. Good afternoon."

Nina, Daniel, Stefan and some of the others stood and began to vacate the room. They congregated in the hallway as they said goodbye to one another.

Nina's heart jolted as Stefan sidled over to where she and Daniel were standing.

"Daniel," Stefan started, "I will come and collect you from your home tomorrow morning at around 8 o'clock if that is appropriate? I trust you are looking forward to your first day at the hospital?"

"Very much," Daniel nodded.

"Excellent!" Stefan said. "I will see you then. Goodbye, Daniel." He seemed to pause for a moment, and then, to Nina's delight he took her hand in his and raised it to his lips. "Goodbye, Nina. It was lovely to see you both." Nina blushed as Stefan's fingers moved against hers and she could feel that he was subtly placing something in her palm. It felt like a folded up piece of parchment. He released her hand and took his leave and Nina watched him walk away, his dark hair shining in the daylight.

Nina and Daniel walked home together, arm in arm, and Daniel spoke at length about everything he was looking forward to at the hospital the following day. Nina listened with interest, but secretly, she was looking forward to going to her bedroom alone so she could read what Stefan had placed in her hand.

At long last, they arrived home and Nina closed the master bedroom door behind her. The parchment was still in her hand, and with shaking hands she unfolded it. Her eyes devoured it while her stomach began to perform somersaults. Stefan's handwriting was slanted yet neat and elegant.

Nina, you look stunningly beautiful today. You are making it very difficult for me to forget what happened last night. If you want to discuss this further, then you know where I will be tomorrow evening. If not, then I understand. Best wishes, S.

CHAPTER VIII

January 1905

Later that night, the wind howled and the rain clattered against the windows of Monroe Manor's master bedroom. The force of the weather was so strong that it woke Nina from her already restless sleep. She turned to look at the other side of the bed. Lucas was not there, of course. She supposed that he would be out all night, and that at this moment, he was probably with somebody else. She scowled to herself but then reminded herself that she intended to do the very same thing the next night. Thoughts of Stefan's note occupied her thoughts. Was it an invitation for sex or merely to talk? Just as Nina resolved to analyse the subtext of the note for the foreseeable future, she sensed movement in the corridor outside the bedroom, and to her dismay, the door opened. It was dark in the room, but Nina recognised Lucas' footsteps and the smell of his cologne. There was more movement as he removed his clothes and climbed into the bed next to her.

"Nina, are you awake?" Lucas crooned, moving his body against hers. His skin and his hair was wet and cold from the harsh weather outside.

"Yes," she whispered. "Why are you back so late?"

"I was playing cards with Stefan and William, and while we were playing I realised that I have been unfair to you lately," he replied, nuzzling her hair and neck and cradling her within his strong arms. Nina could smell whiskey on his breath.

"Did you procure that wisdom from the bottom of the whiskey bottle, darling?" she asked.

He laughed and kissed underneath her right ear. "Perhaps, darling, but it doesn't negate the truth of the matter, nor my sincerity."

His once skilful hands caressed her neck and then moved down to her breasts. Nina could not help but remember how exciting their relationship had been at the beginning, when she was a girl of eighteen. Lucas had been so attentive and he had shown so much interest in her then. She remembered how they used to sneak away from their fathers' *Shrewd Seven* meetings and have secret trysts of their own in the library of Rosethorn Manor. She remembered how Lucas had adored and worshipped her. But now, after nineteen years of marriage, and as a woman of thirty seven, she felt tired and neglected. She knew that a part of her would always love Lucas for giving Daniel to her, but she wondered if she still loved him romantically. He certainly seemed to be trying to earn some of that love back now, she thought, as he rolled her onto her back and positioned himself over her, kissing her neck like she so used to enjoy. Lately, she had felt nothing when they had slept together. No feelings, no excitement.

"I am sorry for how I have treated you recently," Lucas groaned, as he began to have his way.

Nina said nothing but closed her eyes and waited for it to be over. Unbidden images of Stefan's face surfaced in her mind's eye, and suddenly, feelings of desire dared to flare within her. As Lucas' beard grazed the side of her cheek, she found herself imagining that it was Stefan's and her heart soared with longing.

"I will try and be a better husband," Lucas moaned into her ear as he slowed to completion at last. "I love you, Nina," he said.

"I love you too," she whispered back automatically, but in truth, she felt devoid of any emotion.

Lucas sighed, removed himself from the intertwined limbs and bedsheets and rolled away from her, while Nina was overcome with an overwhelming sense of relief. Soon, Lucas fell asleep and his breathing became as deep and heavy as the tumultuous weather outside. Nina cursed everything as she lay awake for the rest of the night, with only her desirous thoughts of Stefan for company. Elsewhere, unbeknownst to Nina, Stefan was lying awake thinking of her.

*

As the clocks chimed eight o'clock the next morning, Nina and Daniel were making their way down the stairs and Harper opened the front door of Monroe Manor to reveal Stefan Sinclair. He was wearing a long, dark coat over his suit and he was carrying his doctor's bag in his right hand. As Nina and Daniel stepped down into the entrance hall, Stefan crossed the threshold and greeted them with a smile.

"Good morning, Daniel… Nina…" he said, his eyes flashing towards Nina for a fraction of a second.

"Good morning," Nina replied hastily, hoping that her face had not betrayed her by blushing. Daniel moved forwards to shake Stefan's hand.

Daniel was wearing a new suit and he had smoothed his hair back with oil. Nina thought that he looked much older than sixteen and she could feel herself getting emotional.

"Good luck on your first day," she said, hugging her son.

"Thank you, mother," he said, grinning at her as she released him.

"Where is Lucas this morning?" Stefan asked politely.

"He is indisposed, I am afraid. I think he drank too much whiskey last night during your card game," Nina replied. She was unable to look Stefan in the eye at the present moment, given her thoughts about him the previous night. "He remains in bed clutching his aching head, but he asked me to wish you good luck, Danny."

"I see," Stefan chuckled. "You start walking Daniel, I just want to tell your mother what you will be doing on your first day. I will catch up."

"Alright, goodbye, mother," Daniel said, and set off on his way.

Nina watched him go, and she felt tears welling up behind her eyes. He was growing up so fast. Where had the time gone? It didn't seem so long ago that he had taken his first steps.

"I hope Daniel does well at the hospital," Nina said.

"He will be fantastic with the patients, I have no doubt," Stefan said. He glanced around to make sure that nobody was looking before kissing Nina's hand.

"I will be home from seven o'clock this evening. I hope that I will see you then," he said quietly, his eyes twinkling with hope.

"You will," Nina whispered back, now able to look into his eyes.

"Wonderful," he replied, and gave her hand a little squeeze, before he, too, set off down the stone pathway.

Nina closed the door behind him and leaned against it for a while with her eyes closed. As more lustful thoughts raced around her brain, she decided that she had better go upstairs and care for her ailing husband.

*

After caressing her husband's hair, fetching him food and water, and massaging his back and shoulders for most of the day, Nina began to feel tired, but the thought of her impending visit to Stefan's house sustained her energy. Daniel had arrived home at around three o'clock in the afternoon, and to Nina's delight, he had thoroughly enjoyed his day at the hospital. He had shadowed Stefan for the day and had even taken care of sick patients. Nina rather thought that she had had a similar day caring for Lucas. As she had watched her husband suffer all day, she felt a slight twinge of guilt for what she was intending to do later that evening. She had been having an intense debate with herself for the greater part of the day. Could she really do this to Lucas? Did she want to become an adulterer? Did she want to start an affair with Stefan and betray Lucas? What would Daniel do if he found out? What would *Lucas* do if he found out? She willed herself to stop having such thoughts. Besides, it could all be for nothing. Perhaps Stefan really did just want to talk. Was it possible that he could feel the same way about her?

At about six o'clock in the evening, Lucas seemed to feel better, and he climbed out of bed and began getting dressed.

"Thank you for caring for me, today, Nina," he said and kissed her on her forehead. "I am going out now, and I don't think I will be back tonight."

"Oh, alright," she said. This suited her very well. "Where are you going?"

"Out," he said blankly.

"With a woman?" Nina asked sternly.

Lucas shrugged his shoulders and began to make his way to the door.

"What about everything you said last night?" Nina cried incredulously. She should have known that his words were too good to be true. *How naïve of me*, she thought bitterly.

"Oh, darling, you should learn not to listen to a man when he is both drunk and in pursuit of sex," Lucas sneered. He was definitely back to his usual self, then.

There was a pause.

"Duly noted, darling," Nina said at last, smiling sweetly, but deep inside, her anger was ricocheting from nerve to nerve.

Lucas looked slightly bemused by her calm and composed façade, but he blew her a kiss and continued on his way. Any guilt or doubt Nina had felt about her intentions that evening were extinguished immediately. She wanted what he had – the freedom to be with whomever he pleased.

*

An hour later, Nina was ready. Her maid, Lottie, had helped her to curl her hair and to plait and pin the sides around the back of her head. Nina had applied her makeup with careful precision, and as the clocks chimed seven, Nina regarded her reflection in the mirror. Her eyes were dark and smoky, her cheeks were soft and rouge, and her lips were painted blood-red. She knew that she looked desirable, but she wondered if Stefan would think so. She was wearing a stylish red dress with a corset that she had borrowed from Lolita. It was sophisticated but, thanks to the corset, her chest looked fuller and bigger than it normally did. To draw attention to it, she had adorned her neck and chest with a silver and ruby necklace. Nina felt breathless as she realised that it was time to leave. She lifted the glass of wine from the dressing table and drained it in one. She definitely did not want to be intoxicated around Stefan again, but she did feel the need to have one glass to stabilise her nerves.

Nina pulled a black cloak around her shoulders and began her journey to Stefan's house. She was barely aware of her surroundings as she walked, due to her ruminations and frenzied thoughts. What would happen when she arrived? What would she say? What would he say? Did he intend to sleep with her or did he merely want to tell her that he couldn't kiss her again? Nina took herself by surprise as she realised that she had arrived at Sinclair Manor. By the time she had knocked on the door with shaking hands, she had convinced herself that Stefan was about to reject her once and for all.

As the door opened, she suppressed a sigh as Stefan smiled at her. He was wearing a white shirt which was unbuttoned at the top, and smart, black trousers.

"Here we are again," he said, smiling. "Come in, and this time, I feel no guilt for offering you a glass of wine."

His fingers brushed the back of her neck as he removed her cloak from her shoulders. She tried not to shudder at his touch, but then realised that she was holding herself tensely. She took a breath to relax herself.

Once again, she followed him to the drawing room. The fire was lit, and he motioned for her to sit down in one of the armchairs.

"How are you doing today, Nina?" he asked, as he handed her a glass of red wine.

Her heart sank. They were back to being formal and polite.

"Fine..." she said. "I believe that Daniel enjoyed the hospital today."

"Oh, yes," Stefan said, smiling again, "He is a natural doctor, Nina. Very caring and much attuned to the needs of others. You should be very proud of him."

Nina nodded. "I am, he will be a fine man." Nina was relieved that Daniel had not inherited his father's coldness.

"Now, I mean no disrespect to Daniel or to you," Stefan continued, "but I did not ask you to come here to talk about your son."

Nina gulped. She braced herself for the rejection that was surely on its way...

"I asked you to come here so we could talk about the other night," he continued.

"Yes..." she started awkwardly.

"As wrong as it was for me to kiss my best friend's wife, Nina, I can't stop thinking about it. And now that you are in front of me, looking more beautiful than ever, I would like nothing more than to do it again."

Nina felt a pang more intense than ever in the pit of her stomach.

"So would I," she confessed, placing her wine glass on the end table next to the chair.

Apparently, that was all the confirmation Stefan needed, because he took her hand gently and guided her to stand before him. As she stood, he took hold of her waist in one hand, and caressed her face with the other. He began showering her neck with intense kisses and Nina closed her eyes and sighed and let herself fall into his embrace. He moved his head so that his nose was barely an inch from hers.

"I don't know why I feel this way, but I do," he whispered.

She put both of her hands on either side of his neck and brought his lips to hers. They kissed for several moments and Nina relished the sensation of his face and his body so close to hers. Her insides tingled as he deepened the kiss, caressing her tongue with his own. While they kissed, he guided them over to the jade settee at the far corner of the room and Nina fell back onto the cushions, pulling him down with her. With Lucas, Nina often felt subdued and constrained when his body was on top of hers, but now with Stefan, she felt the opposite. She felt attractive. She felt powerful. She felt wanted. Stefan pulled the centre seams of her corset until they tore apart in his hands, while she unbuttoned his shirt with equal fervour. They undressed each other feverishly and passionately, all the while, ensuring that no part of the other's body was left untouched by their lips. Nina enjoyed exploring his hitherto unfamiliar body, enjoyed feeling every muscle beneath his skin. Her heart raced as she felt his fingers and lips on her chest. She wrapped her legs around his hips and they gazed at each other for a moment before he brought his body down as close to hers as possible. *This is heaven*, Nina thought. *I have died and gone to heaven...*

CHAPTER IX

January 1905

Daylight streamed in through the drapes of Sinclair Manor's drawing room, causing Nina to stir. She could feel Stefan's bare chest pressed against her back, and his arms were wrapped around her naked body. They were still lying on the sofa, and during the night, he had covered them with a woollen blanket. She felt movement behind her and smiled as she felt Stefan's lips on her neck.

"Good morning, Nina," he said in a throaty voice. Nina could get used to hearing his voice this early in the morning.

"Good morning," she said, twisting her body around so that they were face to face. Her breasts brushed against his chest and she sighed as he rested one hand on her hip and the other on the side of her neck.

Although it was first thing in the morning, Stefan looked more handsome than ever. His hair was elegantly swept back from his face and his dark eyes were alight with a piercing glimmer.

"You are amazing, Nina," he said, caressing her neck and face. "Last night was... phenomenal."

She was taken aback. Even after nineteen years of marriage to Lucas, she had genuinely never wondered about her own sexual prowess before. Obviously, Lucas seemed to enjoy their times together, but for Nina, until now, sex had always been a means to an end.

"As are you," she said, smiling. "I hope that you don't regret it."

He laughed. "Of course not. Do you?"

Nina considered this for a moment. Last night had certainly

been the most erotic and pleasurable night of her life, but now that it had happened, what did it mean for her? Would she remain married to Lucas and continue sleeping with both of them? Would Stefan want an affair with her? Had it been a one-night only arrangement? Her head began to throb with confusion. She did not like to think about the consequences for them should Lucas or William discover what had happened between them the previous night.

"No, I wanted – I *want* – this very much," Nina replied thoughtfully. "But I don't know what it means."

He snaked his arms around her body and pulled her closer to him. She winced as he whispered directly into her ear.

"I don't know what it means either, Nina, but I would very much like to continue seeing you like this, if you would like to…"

"I would like that," Nina said quietly. "But we need to be careful, Stefan. If Lucas or William find out…"

"Ssh, Nina," he crooned. "I would not allow that. This is between us, and us alone."

She sighed with relief. His hands moved down her body and he began to stroke her inner thighs while kissing her neck. After a few moments, she held his head in her hands and pulled his lips towards hers. She ran her hands over his body and then moved her body so that she was sitting up on top of him. Her legs were either side of his hips and he gently cupped her buttocks with his hands.

"Again?" Stefan asked breathlessly.

Nina smiled and moved her face down towards his, capturing his lips with her own.

*

Nina had returned to Monroe Manor shortly before luncheon and to her surprise and relief, Lucas had not yet arrived home. She and Daniel took their places at their dining table while

Harper and the other servants began to serve their meal. Just as Nina took her first bite of chicken, the dining room door opened and Lucas swept towards the table and took his seat at its head.

"Good afternoon, darling," he said, placing a kiss on Nina's cheek.

She regarded her husband with a false smile, and to her disgust, she noticed that there was a red lipstick stain on the edge of his white collar. Nina could not stifle the thought that the shade of the red lipstick clashed horribly with Rosalyn Whittaker's red hair. She really ought to reconsider her choice of makeup.

"Good afternoon, Lucas, I see you have not changed your clothes since last night."

Lucas frowned at her and Daniel shifted uncomfortably in his seat.

"Not now, Nina," he said through gritted teeth. "I hope you had a good evening."

"I certainly did," she said, smiling sweetly. Images of Stefan's face and naked body swam before her eyes. She was thankful that Lucas could not see into her mind, but she reminded herself that he certainly would have no qualms about invading her thoughts if he was able to.

"Good, I'm glad," Lucas said, but his facial expression could not have shown less interest. "How was the hospital, Daniel?"

Nina lost focus as Daniel began to recount his day of volunteer work to his father. She was staring at her plate of food without really seeing it. All she could think about was how much she wanted to see Stefan again, and how good it felt to have a part of her life that was truly hers – a part of her life with which Lucas could not interfere.

"We will be retrieving the crate of guns tomorrow night," Lucas said suddenly, and this brought Nina's attention back to the conversation.

"Oh, Lucas, be careful, won't you?" Nina asked. "And look after Lolita, please."

"I am always careful, Nina," Lucas replied. "And Lolita would slap me before she allowed me to look after her."

Nina smiled to herself. "Perhaps that is true, but she needs to understand that she is more delicate now that she is with child."

"Don't let her hear you saying that," Lucas said, laughing.

"Where will you take the guns?" Nina asked with concern. Despite their marital difficulties, Nina still cared about Lucas' welfare and safety.

"We will pick them up at Millwall, and then deposit them in the cellar of Rosethorn Manor until William appraises them and then he will decide what to do with them, I suppose."

"Will he sell them?"

"Possibly, Nina. I am not sure," Lucas said. He took his last bite of his meal and then set down his cutlery. "Now that we are finished, shall we retire to the drawing room?"

"Yes, darling," Nina said and stood, placing her arm within Lucas'. They walked, arm in arm, towards their drawing room and Daniel followed. For the rest of the afternoon, Lucas and Daniel played cards and Nina sketched and painted at her easel. They drank and laughed together as a family, and it almost felt as comfortable as it did when Daniel was a boy. Almost.

*

Late the following afternoon, Nina held back tears as she kissed her husband at the front door of Monroe Manor. He was going to the Millwall Docks with William and Lolita and the other *Seven* members to retrieve the crate of guns. Nina always felt anxious and apprehensive when Lucas left on *Shrewd Seven* business, and despite their volatile relationship, tonight was no different.

"Please take care," she said, embracing him. He snaked his arms around her waist and kissed her lips gingerly.

"I will. I don't know what time I will be back, but I hope to be with you in bed tonight," he said.

Nina did not know how she felt about this. She stayed silent and kissed him again.

As he left, she closed the door and walked to the drawing room where Lottie had left some wine for her. The large manor felt more empty than usual now Daniel was at the hospital and Lucas had left on business.

Nina and Lucas had spent a long time together over the past day and a half, and they hadn't argued at all. In fact, Nina thought, Lucas had been quite agreeable, and she had actually enjoyed being in his company. Despite this, however, she felt a definite sense of unease because she had not heard from Stefan since she had left his manor the other morning. Perhaps he had grown to regret their night together, after all.

Nina continued to ruminate over such thoughts as she drank one glass of wine after another. The sky began to grow dark outside and she had just decided to continue painting at her easel when there was a knock at the front door of the manor. Who could it be? Daniel and Stefan were at the hospital and Lucas had left for the Docks…

Nina stood and pulled a shawl over her shoulders. As she opened the door and began making her way into the entrance hall, she saw that Harper had opened the large front door.

"Dr Sinclair! How lovely to see you," said Harper.

Nina's heart raced.

"Hello, Harper, I have come to check on Nina now that Lucas has left," Stefan's voice said. Her heart leapt again as Stefan stepped over the threshold and he regarded her with a warm smile.

As Harper quitted the entrance hall, Stefan took Nina's hand in his and raised it to his lips.

"Hello Nina, I have missed you," he whispered.

"And I you," she said breathlessly. "Please, let's go into the drawing room."

Her eyes roved around the entrance hall, checking for stray servants. The last thing she needed was the servants to begin gossiping about them.

She led the way and as she closed the door behind them, Stefan took hold of her hips and turned her to face him. He pressed his body against hers and kissed her lips passionately.

After a few moments he pulled away and said. "I'm sorry, I have just wanted to do that ever since I last saw you."

"You don't need to apologise," Nina said, smiling. "I thought you were at the hospital tonight."

"I was," Stefan said, taking hold of her hand and leading her to one of the settees. "But I left my inferiors in charge because I just had to see you tonight."

Nina blushed.

"I would like to take you out somewhere," he continued.

"Oh really?" she said, surprised.

"Yes," he said, and withdrew two slips of paper from his waistcoat pocket. "I have two tickets to a performance of *Romeo and Juliet* at Haymarket Theatre if you would like to join me."

Her heart soared. She adored Shakespeare's plays. The drawing room's bookshelves were laden with the works of Shakespeare.

"Oh, Stefan, yes of course I would!"

She kissed his lips eagerly and he kissed her back with equal passion, before standing up and breaking the embrace. "As much as I would like to uphold our tradition of sleeping together on drawing room settees, the performance starts soon so we really ought to leave now. There will be plenty of time for kisses afterwards," he said, smiling, and took her hand in his. "Let's go. My carriage is waiting for us outside."

CHAPTER X

January 1905

The ornate golden ceiling, the dancing flames on the glittering chandeliers, the luxurious scarlet seats, the astounding costumes and makeup, and the breath-taking, mellifluous music from the orchestra... Nina was in complete awe of everything around her at the Haymarket Theatre. Stefan had paid for their own private seats in a box close to the right-hand side of the stage, and he had held her in his arms during the more emotionally intense moments of the play.

Of course, all good things must come to an end, thought Nina as the actor portraying Prince uttered the final lines of the play: "For never was a story of more woe than this of Juliet and her Romeo."

A colossal, scarlet curtain descended from the rafters and obscured the stage and the actors. The audience applauded and cheered loudly, and Nina wiped away her tears. It had been a sensational performance. She turned to Stefan who was beaming back at her.

"That was amazing, Stefan, thank you so much for this special night," she said, placing a kiss on his cheek.

"It was my pleasure, Nina, I am glad that you enjoyed it," he replied and took her hand in his. "Come now, let's go somewhere for a drink." He stood and Nina followed suit.

They made their way out of the box and waded through the masses of elegantly dressed theatre-goers, until at last, they reached the busy London street outside. The air was crisp and the gentle wind ruffled Stefan's dark, wavy hair as they walked hand in hand. Both the moonlight and the oil lamps from the nearby buildings illuminated their path. Nina shivered and drew her scarf closer to her exposed neck, and when Stefan noticed this, he stopped, took off his own coat and draped it around her shoulders.

"Stefan, don't be ridiculous!" Nina protested. "I already have my own coat, and you'll catch your death in this weather!"

"You have warmed this cold heart of mine, Nina," he joked, "So I don't think it is possible for me to feel the cold."

Nina rolled her eyes in a jovial manner. "If you insist," she said, grinning at him.

They walked down narrow, cobbled streets until at last, Stefan led them towards an elegant little building. Its exterior stone walls were adorned with brass oil lamps and several hanging baskets containing red and white roses.

"I know how much you like wine, Nina, so I thought I would bring you to this little wine bar. I know the owner and he has said that he will provide us with our own private snug."

Nina smiled. It sounded perfect. As they walked inside, the heat emanating from the crackling fire warmed Nina's face and it was gratefully received. The room was cosy and beautifully decorated. The seats were gold and black and the dark, marble bar itself was so well-polished that it positively gleamed. The bearded man behind the bar greeted them with a wide smile.

"Ah, Stefan! Good to see you," he said. "What can I get for you and this lovely lady?"

"Two red wines, if you please," Stefan replied. Nina stayed silent. She was glad that he had not introduced her by name. Anybody could be listening, after all.

Nina's eyes roved around the room as she heard the wine tinkling at the bottom of the glasses as it was poured. The bar was moderately busy, but she did not see anybody that she recognised.

The barman carried the two glasses of wine over to a door at the far side of the bar. He opened the door to reveal a snug complete with a large, brown settee and an oak table.

"There you are, Stefan," the barman said, handing the glasses to him. "There is a little hatch on the wall that you can open if you would like to request some more drinks."

"Thanks, Charlie," Stefan said and let Nina pass before closing the door.

Nina took a seat and removed her two coats and her scarf. Stefan sat down next to her and handed her one of the glasses of wine.

They talked, they laughed, and they drank. Nina did not know how long they had been sitting together in the snug, but she did know that she was having an extremely enjoyable night with Stefan. Being with him was simply effortless. The conversation flowed easily and they shared many common interests; notably art and literature. After two bottles of red wine, with their inhibitions lowered, their conversation became increasingly intimate and unreserved.

"Do you know, Stefan, that until you and I started… *this*… I had only ever been with Lucas?" Nina said, giggling.

"Lucky bastard, having you all to himself," Stefan teased.

Nina pushed him jokingly.

"Watch your language, Stefan Sinclair," She said with a mock pout.

"In all seriousness, though, I find it hard to believe, Nina," Stefan slurred. "Look at you, you are beautiful."

Nina felt the heat rising in her cheeks. She shrugged. "Lucas and I started courting when I was very young, and until you, nobody has ever expressed an interest in me."

"But I bet that men admired you from afar," Stefan went on. "I know that I certainly did."

"You did?" Nina asked, genuinely shocked.

"Of course, Nina. I remember the first time I noticed your beauty, actually," Stefan said thoughtfully. "It was Daniel's christening at the Parish, and I remember you were wearing a stunning dark blue dress and you had your hair up, and you were wearing a matching fascinator. You looked so incredibly nervous as you held Daniel over the baptismal font. It was endearing. And that was the first time I thought 'She is gorgeous'. But I kept quiet, of course."

Nina stared at him in wonder. She watched as he took another sip of wine and she felt her heart pounding against her chest.

"All these years..." she started.

"Yes, and now all those years of silent admiration have been worth it in the end," he said, caressing her cheek.

"What about you, Stefan?" she began, gazing deeply into his eyes.

"What about me?" he whispered.

"How is it that you are without a wife? Have you ever been in love? How many women have you been with?"

"So many questions," Stefan said, smiling. "I don't know exactly how many women I have been with... possibly ten? Maybe more... And the answers to your other questions are stories for another time, I'm afraid. I wouldn't want to bore you with all of the details now on this perfect night."

For a fraction of a second, Nina sensed heavy emotion behind Stefan's eyes, but her view of this became obscured as he began kissing her neck. She clutched his back fervently and melted at his touch.

"I want you now, Nina," Stefan groaned into her ear.

"What, here?" she asked.

"Yes, here and now," he replied.

He kissed her lips and placed his hands on the back of her neck, running them through her blonde, curled hair. Nina's stomach lurched as he began clawing at the skirts of her dress, lifting up all of the layers until his hands reached her bare skin. She unbuttoned the front of his trousers skilfully as they kissed and pulled them down so that she could caress his bare thighs and buttocks. Stefan pushed her softly down onto the settee and hoisted himself into a kneeling position above her. He took hold of her bare legs and prised them apart gently, before moving his body on top of hers and kissing her lips and face passionately.

"My Nina," he moaned into her ear as they became lost in the passion of the moment.

"You are my Nina," he said again, breathlessly, and Nina felt her body explode with desire.

*

An hour later, at midnight, Stefan kissed Nina goodbye at the front door of Monroe Manor.

"Goodnight, Nina," he said. "I am afraid I must return to the hospital to check on my patients. Daniel will be home now, granted he might be asleep…And Lucas and the others will be back from their assignment soon, no doubt. I have had a wonderful night, Nina."

"Thank you, Stefan, tonight was… perfect," she said, and entered the Manor, closing the door behind her. She made her way through the vast hallway and ascended the grand staircase, with a view to climbing into bed and dreaming of Stefan all night.

At last, she slipped on her nightwear and rested her head on her pillow. Lottie had clearly slipped the brass bed warmer under the duvet earlier that night because the bed was so warm that Nina fell asleep almost instantly.

*

The grandfather clock in the hallway outside of the bedroom chimed four times, but that was not what had woken her from her deep slumber. Somebody was sitting on the edge of the bed and was shaking her frantically. They had lit the oil lamp on the bedside table.

"Nina, for God's sake, wake up!" a woman's voice cried.

As Nina stirred, she recognised the voice to be that of her sister, Lolita. As she opened her eyes, the light from the oil lamp threw her sister's face into sharp relief. Her eyes were popping wildly, and her dark, curly hair was standing on end. Nina noticed that Lolita had a gash on her cheek and her lip was bleeding.

"Oh my god, Lolita!" Nina cried and sat up in bed.

"Nina! There was a blunder with the raid! The police came and seized the guns! They have arrested Lucas and Robert and the other men!"

Nina's heart jolted violently.

"They have been arrested? Are they at the police station?"

"Yes, they took them away right before my eyes," Lolita said.

"How did you get away?" Nina asked quietly, putting her hands over her eyes and running her hands through her hair.

"William seized me and took me to safety," Lolita said proudly in a voice heavy with emotion. "He saved me..."

Nina rolled her eyes at her sister before her panic about Lucas set in. "What am I going to do now that they have Lucas? Will William be able to rescue him from police custody?"

"I don't think so," Lolita said weakly. "It turns out the police commissioner that William has been blackmailing died a few days ago, so William has... lost his control over the police..." Lolita's bottom lip began to tremble.

Nina clapped her hand to her mouth. The world around her seemed to come to a crashing halt. A thousand thoughts soared around Nina's frantic mind. Would Lucas be charged and sent to prison? What would become of her and Daniel? What did the loss of William's control over the police mean for *The Shrewd Seven*? Nina closed her eyes as tears started to fall from them. Lolita held her in her arms like she had done so many times when they were young girls.

"It'll be okay, Nina," Lolita crooned. "William will think of something, you mark my words."

CHAPTER XI

March 1905

Two months had passed since the failed gun crate heist. Lucas and the other men had been found guilty by the court, and had been sentenced to two years in prison. In the days following the men's arrest, in his anger and despondence, William had ordered that all of the remaining *Shrewd Seven* members and their families should move into Sinclair Manor for their safety and protection. Rosethorn Manor was now compromised, as were the houses of the other men that had taken part in the raid. Despite Lolita's promise to Nina, William had not yet managed to secure the men's release.

Now that Stefan's house was full of people, it had been extremely difficult for Nina and Stefan to resume their relationship. They had taken to meeting in Stefan's bedroom in the middle of the night when everyone was asleep, or else in his office at the hospital. Lolita, now six months pregnant, with her ever-expanding midsection, was becoming increasingly irritable and emotional. William had forbidden her from taking part in any of the *Seven*'s field activities due to her condition. Since the gun crate heist, the remaining men had completed a handful of minor raids successfully, but they had had to employ certain levels of stealth and care, due to the new and improved police presence.

On one particular spring evening, William had arranged for a renowned group of pianists and violinists to perform in the ballroom at Sinclair Manor, and had hired staff to serve food and drinks. For Nina, it seemed strange to attend a ball without her husband. She wondered what Lucas was doing now, and she worried daily about his welfare.

As the ball drew closer, Nina and Lolita dressed together in the guest room that had been assigned to Nina (not that she actually slept there very often).

"Oh, Nina, none of my dresses fit properly now!" wailed Lolita as she contemplated her appearance in the mirror beside the dressing table.

"They will if you loosen your corset. Anyway, a tight corset can't be good for the baby. Here…" Nina said, adjusting the laces accordingly.

Lolita let out a deep breath. "Ah, thank you, Nina, that is much better. Are you sure that I don't look huge?"

Nina rolled her eyes.

"You can hardly see your bump under the many layers of your dress, Lolita. You look lovely, as always."

Lolita turned and smiled. Pregnancy seemed to give her skin a fresh glow. Her dark curls were pinned into a sophisticated up-do and her makeup was smokey and breath-taking, as always. Her deep plum coloured dress was beautiful and despite the looseness of her corset, her chest heaved over the top of the material of the dress.

"One good thing about being pregnant is that my breasts are enormous!" Lolita laughed.

Nina smirked. "I can see that. And I think that everyone else can, too. Will you help me to fasten this dress, please?"

Nina breathed in deeply as Lolita fastened her emerald corset and she regarded her reflection in the mirror. Her eyes were smoky like Lolita's and she had painted her lips deepest crimson. Her blonde curls were pinned up at the sides of her head, allowing the rest of her hair to cascade down her shoulders and back.

Lolita stood back and looked at Nina.

"You look beautiful, Nina. Do you think *she* will grow up to be beautiful?"

Nina looked thoroughly nonplussed as to who *she* was, but then noticed that Lolita had placed her hand over her stomach.

"She?" Nina asked blankly. "How can you know that?"

"I just know," Lolita said. "She just *feels* like a girl. Do you think she will be beautiful?"

"Well, you are beautiful, so I would say so, but I would have to know what the father looks like to make a conclusive judgment…" Nina teased.

"For God's sake, Nina, stop trying to make me tell you," Lolita snapped. "I have already told you that I am not sure who it is."

"I am teasing, Lolita," Nina said as she sprayed perfume over her sister. "Have you thought of any names for the little one yet?"

"No," Lolita replied. "I think I need to wait until I see her."

Nina took her elder sister's arm and the two women walked out of the room, across the hall, and down the stairs.

As they entered the ballroom together, beautiful music filled Nina's ears. The remaining *Seven* men and their families had already begun their festivities. Although there were only four men missing – Lucas, Robert, Robert's brother Oscar and Stefan's brother Harry – the gathering seemed so much smaller than usual, and the ratio of women to men seemed to be much larger.

The room was vast and spectacular. The panelled walls were cream and lustrous, and the marble floor gleamed as the chandeliers glittered from the ceiling. Some of the people were already dancing, but Lolita led Nina over to the table of drinks. Noticing that there were copious varieties of wine on offer, Nina was glad to follow. Just as one of the serving girls began to pour a glass of wine for Nina, she jumped as she heard William's voice behind her.

"-plenty of women here for you to choose from tonight, Stefan," William was saying. His words were slurred and as Nina turned to look at William and Stefan, she could see that William's eyes were uncharacteristically glazed and unfocused. She suspected that he had already over-indulged on alcohol.

Stefan looked at Nina for a fraction of a second before replying.

"I am not interested, William…"

"Oh, come off it, Stefan!" said William, roaring with laughter. "You could have a go at Rosalyn now that Lucas isn't here, eh? Or what about her sister, Lucy? She is looking very well tonight."

"Not for me, thank you. You could try, though." Stefan replied dryly. Beside her, Nina could feel the silent rage emanating from Lolita at the very idea of William with another woman.

"Oh, Stefan, you can't still be pining after your woman, can you, after all these years?" William said, clapping Stefan on the back. "Come on, now, there are lots of serving girls here that are nice to look at. Like I always say, fuck whoever you want, just don't go falling in love with anyone who isn't a part of the *Seven*, eh?"

Nina's heart began beating wildly against her chest. Who was the woman that William was referring to? Stefan flashed Nina a look which plainly said *"I shall explain later,"* before he excused himself and walked away to the dancefloor, out of Nina's sight.

William, too, disappeared, probably to heckle one of the other men, so Nina and Lolita proceeded to drink their wine and gossip at the edge of the dancefloor.

*

After the ball had ended and everyone had gone to bed, Nina roamed the dark upstairs hallways of Sinclair Manor, trying to locate Stefan's bedroom. The ball had been enjoyable. Lolita had disappeared halfway through the night, so Nina had instead socialised with some of the other women in attendance. Despite Nina's dislike of Rosalyn Whittaker, Rosalyn's sister Lucy was very agreeable and she and Nina had drank and danced together for a large portion of the night. Stefan had been drinking quietly with some of the men at a table, and as Nina had glanced over at him, he had given her a shadow of a wink and a smile. It would have been unwise for them to spend time together at the ball, with so many prying eyes, but Nina knew that she was welcome in his bedroom afterwards. If she could find it, that was. In the semi-darkness, and with her alcohol-infused mind, the bedroom doors all looked identical.

As Nina walked along the hallway, a door opened a short distance ahead of her and a woman stumbled out, closing the door haphazardly behind her. Nina immediately recognised the door as the door to William's room. As Nina drew closer, her eyes fell on the shadowy figure of the woman. The nearby oil lamp illuminated the woman's features and Nina realised that the woman was in fact, Lolita.

Both women were as intoxicated as each other, and both locked eyes on one another at the same moment.

"Nina!" Lolita cried, "What are you doing here?"

"I could ask you the same question, Lolita," Nina whispered. "Did you just leave William's bedroom?"

"What is it to you?" Lolita drawled, and then her eyes narrowed and Nina could sense an accusatory tone in her voice. "Are you hoping to go in there too?"

"What? No!" Nina cried. "I was trying to find my own room…"

Lolita let out a sigh of relief. "Oh. Well, goodnight, sister." She made to walk away but Nina called to her.

"Lolita, wait! What were you doing in William's bedroom?" Nina asked. She had always suspected that Lolita and William were sleeping together, but her sister had never actually confirmed it.

"Well, I was in his bed…" Lolita began shiftily.

"So you were in the bed and where was William?" Nina asked, goading her sister, and hoping for a confession.

"William was with me…" Lolita said cautiously, glancing at the door, as though concerned that William could hear them.

"But not… surely not… sexually?" Nina asked in a voice of mock-astonishment, giggling at the impatient glare on her sister's face.

"For fuck's sake, Nina, yes, sexually," Lolita hissed. "There, are you happy? I said it."

"That is all I wanted to know, dear sister. Goodnight," Nina said, and with that, the two drunken women went their separate ways.

At last, as Nina continued down the hallway, she reached Stefan's bedroom door. She pushed it open and found Stefan sitting upright in bed. The oil lamp on his dresser was flickering, illuminating his handsome eyes and his prominent cheekbones.

"There you are, Nina," he said softly, appraising her. "I was just about to assume that you weren't coming tonight."

Nina removed her clothes and climbed into the bed beside him.

"Guess what?" Nina said, looking at Stefan.

"Go on, tell me," he said, placing down the book he had been reading.

"I have just seen Lolita leaving William's bedroom."

Stefan smiled and raised an eyebrow. "Does that surprise you, Nina?"

"Well, no. I mean, I always thought that it was happening, but she just confirmed it!" Nina said feverishly.

"How enthralling," Stefan said jokingly. "That really isn't news to me, Nina. Anyway, I am glad that you came here tonight, because it was so difficult not to kiss you at the ball. You looked so incredibly beautiful, and you were very hard to resist."

He moved his face closer to hers, and started kissing her neck, but Nina put her hand in front of his face.

"Excuse me, Stefan Sinclair, before you try to seduce me, I have a bone to pick with you," Nina slurred.

"Oh," Stefan said flatly. He seemed to know what she was referring to. "You want to know what William was talking to me about, don't you?"

"Yes," Nina replied. "Who is the woman that you are supposedly pining for?"

Stefan took a deep breath as if he was steeling himself for something very profound.

"A while ago you asked me if I had ever been in love, and I said that I would tell you another time. I guess now is the time to tell you."

Nina nodded.

"The first thing you need to know, Nina, is that it was a long time ago," Stefan began. "I was a young man of maybe twenty-two. Lucas and I used to frequent the inn *The Sapphire* and there was a barmaid there. Her name was Lara Beckett. I... grew quite fond of her..."

"I see," Nina said. "What happened?"

"Well, I asked William if I could marry her and he point-blank refused to even acknowledge my feelings for her. He said what he said tonight, that I could fuck whoever I wanted, but under no circumstances was I to fall in love with anybody that was not a part of the *Seven*."

Nina noticed that Stefan's features had contorted. He looked emotional and vulnerable and Nina put her arms around him.

"I am sorry, Stefan, I never knew! Did Lucas know this?"

"Lucas and William knew of my feelings for Lara, but nobody knows what I did next," Stefan continued. "I am going to tell you, Nina. Firstly because I trust you, and secondly because I don't think you will let me get away with only telling you half of a story."

Nina smiled. "You can tell me if you want to, Stefan. You know that I won't tell a soul."

"Yes, Nina, it is very important that you keep this to yourself," Stefan whispered. "You see, despite William's disapproval, I married her. I married her in secret. Nobody knows this."

"Oh, Stefan!" Nina was speechless. Her heart ached for the torment that her lover must have faced all those years ago. And her heart ached now as she looked at Stefan's pained features. Nina could see that there were tears building behind Stefan's eyes, but he was able to contain his emotions.

"So yes, we were married, and lived apart, and then a year later, she died of consumption. So now you know…" Stefan said with an air of finality.

Tears fell from Nina's eyes and she sobbed into Stefan's shoulder.

"I am so sorry that you had to go through that and keep it to yourself," Nina said, though her voice was muffled.

"It is alright, Nina, it was a long time ago…" Stefan said and stroked her hair. "Time has diluted the worst of my grief. Now, nobody knows that Lara and I were married, but ever since William rebuffed my feelings for Lara, I have kept all of my romantic relationships away from prying eyes. Naturally, William has always been very… *preoccupied*… with my romantic life, as you saw tonight. Over the years, he has even arranged meetings with women for me, probably hoping that I will get married to somebody that he approves of…"

Nina looked up from Stefan's shoulder and gazed into his eyes which were still laden with emotion. She was incredibly touched that he had shared this with her.

"Thank you for telling me, Stefan," she whispered. "I won't tell anybody. It means a lot that you would trust me with this."

She caressed his neck and kissed his cheek softly. He closed his eyes and held her in his arms, his hands stroking her body. Just before Nina fell asleep with her head on Stefan's chest, she realised that her romantic feelings for Stefan had deepened drastically over the past hour…

CHAPTER XII

March 1905

"Nina, I need you to find a way to get me out of this wretched place," Lucas said in a hollow voice.

Nina and Daniel had been permitted by the authorities to visit Lucas in prison, and the experience was truly horrifying for Nina. The prison was dilapidated with its damp, grey walls and its hard-backed, scratched wooden chairs. Lucas' face was gaunt and unshaven, and his clothes were ragged and unkempt. He seemed to be thoroughly depressed and despondent - he was not his usual, pompous self. Nina's heart broke to see her husband in such a decrepit state.

"I will ask William, darling, I promise," Nina said, tears obscuring her vision. She reached across the table and took hold of his hand, which felt rough and clammy.

"No contact," said the stern voice of one of the prison officers beside them.

Nina released Lucas' hand hastily.

"I think that William is angry with me for failing him," Lucas said quietly. "But please tell me that you will try your best to make him see sense. I cannot go on in here, Nina, it is truly awful."

Nina blinked and tears rolled down her cheeks.

"I will try, darling. I will try my very best."

*

Later that night, Nina was drinking wine and smoking one cigarette after another in her guest bedroom, when Stefan entered the room.

"Good evening, Nina," he called, closing the door behind her.

"How was the hospital?" Nina asked.

"Fine, the same as always, really," Stefan replied, and sat down on the bed beside her. "What is the matter, sweetheart? You don't seem yourself."

He kissed her on the cheek and put his arm around her.

"Daniel and I went to visit Lucas at the prison today," Nina began.

"I see," Stefan said. "How is he doing?"

"It is awful in there, Stefan. Lucas seems to be really suffering. I feel terrible for him." Nina said, twisting her hands together.

"I cannot imagine what he must be going through," Stefan said, shaking his head at the thought. "Please try and put it out of your mind, Nina. I am sure that William will have a plan for him."

"So you and Lolita seem to think, but I don't think that William is particularly concerned about the men!" Nina cried, with a note of hysteria in her voice.

"I cannot deny that William is angry with them," Stefan said, stroking Nina's hair. "But I know that he will come around, darling, we just have to be patient."

Nina closed her eyes and buried her face in Stefan's chest.

"Am I a terrible person, Stefan?" she mumbled.

Stefan took hold of her shoulders and lifted her head up to look at him.

"Now, why on earth would you say that?" he asked quietly.

"Because Lucas is suffering terribly in prison and I am sleeping with you…"

Stefan fell silent for a few moments.

"Would you like to stop?" he asked seriously. "I would understand if you did, Nina."

"No, of course not!" Nina cried. "Being with you is incredible, Stefan. You have made me happier than I have been in a long, long time. I just can't help but feel guilty…"

"That is only natural, Nina," Stefan said reassuringly. "You are such a kind-natured person, and that is one of the many things that I like about you."

"Thank you," Nina said, and kissed him on the forehead. "I'm not a fool, Stefan. I know that if Lucas were here now, he would probably be sleeping around as usual, but I still feel guilty – you should have seen how dejected he looked. It was awful."

"I know," Stefan said and he took her in his arms again. He kissed her neck and her lips hungrily, and she held his neck with her hands as she kissed him back.

"I like kissing you," Stefan breathed in between kisses.

"I like kissing you, too," Nina said breathlessly.

Stefan deepened the kisses and pushed Nina gently so that she fell back on to the bed. He climbed on top of her, tore open her corset and began kissing her chest and breasts.

"I like your body," he said, removing her dress and kissing every bare inch of her skin.

"I like your body too," Nina whispered, as she unbuttoned his shirt and trousers and tossed them aside. As they kissed, Nina ran her hands down the length of his muscular and now familiar body.

"You are amazing…" Stefan moaned, as Nina wrapped her legs around his torso, guiding him towards her.

"So are you…" Nina moaned back. She clutched his back so passionately that she left nail marks on his skin…

*

The following morning, Nina and Stefan awoke early and spent an hour or two talking and cuddling in bed, before Stefan decided that he had better go to his own bedroom, so as not to rouse suspicion amongst the *Seven* members. Five minutes after Stefan had left, there was a knock at the door.

"Yes?" asked Nina, wondering who on earth would want to bother her this early in the morning. It was a good thing that Stefan had left the room when he did.

"It's me," called Lolita's voice through the wood. "Can I come in?"

"I suppose so," Nina called back.

Lolita entered the room. She was wearing a dark night dress and she had tied her unruly dark curls into a messy bun on top of her head. She strode towards the bed with military precision.

"You might have taken the time to brush your hair, Lolita," laughed Nina.

"Shut up and feel my stomach," Lolita commanded.

Nina placed her hand to her sister's stomach and she felt the baby kicking against her palm.

"Oh my goodness, Lolita! This is wonderful!" Nina squealed with excitement.

"So is she supposed to be doing that, then?" asked Lolita quizzically. "I mean I know that you're supposed to feel them moving, but I didn't think it would be so..." She grimaced as the baby kicked again. "...forceful."

"Yes, yes, it is perfectly normal, Lolita," Nina said, smiling. "You have got a feisty baby there. Just like her mother..."

Lolita beamed at her. "I hope she is like me..."

The two sisters sat together for a few moments, feeling the baby kicking and talking together.

After the baby's kicks had subsided, Nina told Lolita about her visit to the prison the previous day.

"So Lucas asked me if there was any way that William could release them..." Nina finished, gazing imploringly into her sister's dark eyes.

Lolita shifted uncomfortably.

"William is very angry with Lucas," Lolita began. "Very angry."

Nina gulped.

"He says that he lost out on hundreds of pounds when the guns were seized by the police," Lolita continued. "Nevertheless, two months have passed now, so I can ask him for you, if you like."

"Would you, Lolita? Thank you!" Nina cried and threw her arms around her sister.

Lolita hugged her back. "Please don't get your hopes up, though, Nina. As you know, William is a very proud and resolute man. This is a testament to how much I care for you, because for one thing, I dislike Lucas, and for another thing, I am quite happy that Robert is locked up... It suits me very well."

Nina laughed into her sister's shoulder.

*

As the clocks chimed six, the remaining *Seven* members and their families took their seats at the dining table at Sinclair Manor. William had ordered the servants from his manor to come to Stefan's house and prepare the evening meal each day. Nina stared woefully at Lucas' empty chair beside her, and then looked across the table and caught Stefan's gaze. He looked around to make sure that nobody else was looking before blowing her a silent and discreet kiss with his hand. Nina smiled to herself.

As always, the meal was delicious. Nina had indulged in roast turkey and potatoes and vegetables, and had enjoyed talking with Daniel about his exploits at the hospital. Stefan had even joined in on the conversation, boasting about Daniel's abilities. Nina always seemed to blush when he spoke to her in front of others, which she knew was dangerous, but she just could not seem to help it. As usual, Lolita and William were whispering and laughing together, and the other members were engaging in their usual gossip and conversation. After the meal, William addressed the table, as he always did.

"I hope you enjoyed the meal tonight, everyone," he began. "Let me begin by announcing that one of my accomplices in Birmingham has assured me that he found the traitor Thomas Whittaker and his wife and daughter yesterday."

Nina's stomach lurched uncomfortably. What were they doing in Birmingham? Did they escape from William's accomplice? She tried to catch Lolita's eye, but Lolita was staring down at her knees. The rest of the group remained silent with bated breath.

"My accomplice tells me that he killed Thomas, but that his wife and daughter escaped," William continued.

Nina suddenly felt extremely nauseous, so she started to massage her stomach with her left hand. Under the table, Daniel clasped her other hand and gave it a little squeeze.

"No matter, perhaps it is for the best that Evangeline and Myrcella live with the guilt of their treachery…" William laughed pompously to himself.

At last, Lolita looked up at Nina and her expression was unreadable, though Nina thought that her eyes looked watery. Lolita rested her chin on her knuckles and stared into nothingness.

Nina could not believe what she was hearing. She felt a rush of empathy for her sister and she wondered how on earth Evangeline and Myrcella must be feeling. She closed her eyes and in her mind, she said a prayer for them. When she opened her eyes, she noticed that Stefan was watching her with an expression of mingled concern and pity. She looked away and tried to block William's words out of her mind. But alas, she could not.

"Now to business," William continued. "A couple of my men on Fleet Street tell me that there is a glass box full of jewels at the jewellers' that might be of interest to us. We could take the box, bring it here and keep it safe until I can find a buyer for the contents."

A few of the men cheered in agreement.

William sneered as he spoke his next words. "Now, I think that it is about time that young Daniel here took on an assignment. Daniel, how do you feel about being the Bouncer while the others do the swiping?"

Nina opened her mouth in horror, but she did not dare to speak a word of indignation. Her son nodded apprehensively and William patted him on the back.

"Good lad!" William cried. "So that's decided. Daniel will take the lead. Let's hope that you are more competent than your father, eh?"

He and the other men laughed. But Nina, Lolita, Daniel and Stefan remained silent. Was there no end to William's torment?

CHAPTER XIII

April 1905

A week had passed, and preparations were well underway for the *Seven's* upcoming jewellery theft. Much to Nina's dismay, Daniel had been required to attend daily planning meetings with William and the other men. Each time that Daniel had left the meeting room, Nina had noticed that he looked paler than normal. She believed that Daniel was quietly terrified of leading the heist, despite his repeated insistences that he was excited to prove himself as a worthy member of the *Seven*.

Lolita and Nina were sitting together in the drawing room of Sinclair Manor on the day before the jewellery theft was to take place. It was a grey and rainy afternoon, and the men were currently engaged in another of their planning meetings. Lolita was distraught because she was not permitted to take part.

"I'm bored, Nina," Lolita wailed, tossing the book she had been reading aside. "How do you entertain yourself all day?"

"You just need to find an activity that you enjoy," Nina said, surveying her sister over the top of her painting easel, which Stefan had delivered from Monroe Manor. "I enjoy painting, and when I paint the hours just seem to dwindle away."

"I enjoy planning the *Shrewd Seven* heists!" Lolita cried. "But thanks to her-" She pointed at her ever-expanding midsection. "- I have to sit in here like a *lady*. I hate it! Why does William treat me like an invalid now?"

Nina chuckled. "You are not an invalid, you just can't behave like you would normally, because fighting and getting into trouble is not good for the baby. Please try and cheer up. Your melancholy mood is not good for her, either."

Lolita pouted, and just as Nina's paintbrush touched the canvas again, the drawing room door swung open. William was wearing a dark suit and waistcoat, and his eyes were alight with malice.

"William!" Lolita cried, turning around in her chair. "How was the meeting? How are the plans for the-?"

William held up a hand to silence her.

"I will talk to you later, Lolita," he said bluntly. "For now, I would like a private word with your sister, if you would be so kind as to leave us..."

Nina's heart jolted, and Lolita's mouth fell open.

"Why?" Lolita asked, narrowing her eyes suspiciously.

"There are some things that I would like to discuss with Nina," said William.

Lolita pouted again and swept out of the room, turning to glare at them as she closed the door behind her. If Nina knew her sister, Lolita would have her ear pressed against the door, and she would be straining to listen to the entirety of their conversation.

"Good afternoon, William," Nina began tentatively. She put down her paintbrush and took a seat in one of the nearby armchairs. "What would you like to discuss with me?"

William smiled at her, but Nina noticed that his smile did not quite meet his menacing eyes.

"I believe that you have been enquiring about my intentions to release your husband and the other men from prison," William began.

"Yes..." Nina replied awkwardly. "I miss Lucas terribly..."

William walked towards Nina and put his hands on either arm of her chair. He leant forward so that his face was mere inches from hers, and when he spoke again, his voice was barely more than a cold whisper.

"Your husband has disappointed me greatly, and he will stay in prison until such time that I have use for him again. Do I make myself clear?"

Nina felt scared, but she did not want to give William the satisfaction of appearing that way, so she looked directly and bravely into his eyes. "Yes," she said.

"Begging Lolita and Daniel to speak with me on your behalf... How cowardly of you," he sneered.

"I am not a coward," Nina said quietly, still determined not to break his gaze.

William laughed again. "If you weren't Lolita's sister, I would strike you for your insolence," he said, baring his teeth.

Nina said nothing but continued to look up at him.

"Let us hope that nothing untoward happens to Daniel on his first real assignment. I would *hate* to see you suffer more than you are suffering now," William continued.

"My Daniel will be fine," Nina said, more to convince herself than to convince William. "He is strong and brave."

"We shall see," William said. "Now don't ever presume to ask others about my plans again, Nina. You are not included in the *Seven*'s business. You are Lucas' wife. Remember your place."

He released the arms of Nina's chair and strode out of the room. As he pushed the door open, the door collided with Lolita, who, true to form, had been eavesdropping outside of the room. She squealed and stood aside for William to pass.

"For God's sake, Lolita! I do not want to fuck your sister, so you don't need to eavesdrop on our conversation!" William growled and continued on his way.

Lolita followed him like a puppy.

"I wasn't..." she began haughtily, but Nina could not hear the rest of their conversation as the door closed behind them.

Nina let out a deep breath, closed her eyes, loosened her shoulders, and unclenched her fists and jaw. No man had ever before inspired such fear in her…

*

Later that night, Nina and Stefan were lying in bed together. Nina's head was resting on Stefan's chest and his strong arms were holding her close to him.

"William spoke to me today," Nina said.

"Oh?" Stefan asked sleepily.

"Yes. He told me that I was to stop asking people about his plans, and he said that if I wasn't Lolita's sister, he would have hit me…"

Talking about William with Stefan was unknown territory for Nina. Nina wondered what Stefan's reaction to this would be, considering William was the leader of the *Seven*. Nevertheless, Nina trusted Stefan, and she knew that anything she said to him would remain between them.

"Did he now?" Stefan said. "Believe me, Nina, if he had hit you, then I would have hit him ten times as hard."

Nina smiled. "What, you would have hit your *Master* for me?"

"He is not my *Master*," Stefan said. "He is the leader of the *Seven*, but he is just a man, Nina. And no man that I know hits a woman and gets away with it. Especially if it was a woman that I cared for."

Nina's insides writhed with pleasure. *A woman that I cared for…*

"Anyway, I am scared, Stefan," Nina said. "I am scared for Daniel tomorrow. What if something goes wrong and Daniel gets captured and sent to prison like Lucas?"

"Nina, I will be there," Stefan began softly. "I will see that Daniel comes to no harm."

"He is too young to be leading a heist like that, Stefan. He has no experience - he is just a boy!" Nina cried. She could feel her emotions rising in her throat.

"Nina, ssh," Stefan said soothingly, stroking her hair. "Did you really think that I would let your son lead the raid tomorrow?"

"What? But William said - " Nina began.

"Yes, William wants Daniel to lead, but I have spoken with Daniel. We have a secret arrangement that I will lead the raid. William will not be there, so what William does not know will not hurt him…"

Nina's emotions soared around her body like wildfire.

"Oh, Stefan!" she squealed and sat up to look at him. "Will you protect him?"

"Of course, Nina," Stefan said and leaned forwards to kiss her lips.

She wrapped her arms around his body and pulled him closer to her.

"Thank you, thank you," Nina whispered into his ear between kisses.

Stefan began kissing her neck and chest, and then Nina's heart lurched as his head disappeared beneath the covers and she felt his hot breath on her skin. His lips brushed against her stomach and then she felt his lips and tongue on her inner thighs. She held his head in his hands and threw her head back against the pillows, moaning with pleasure as he left no part of her body untouched by his soft lips…

CHAPTER XIV

April 1905

Stefan, Daniel, and the other men had successfully retrieved the glass case of jewellery, and William had ordered that Lolita should keep it safe in her room. Lolita, delighted at the prospect of assisting William and the *Seven*, had gleefully accepted, and she had swelled with pride when William had told the other members of the jewellery's current whereabouts.

In celebration of the raid's success, William had organised a party for the *Seven* members and their families. That evening, there was a distinct air of triumph in the ballroom of Sinclair Manor. William was drunk and he was boasting of the *Seven's* prowess to everybody in his general vicinity. He had Lolita on his arm, and every so often, he would turn and kiss her cheek. Lolita was wearing a dark blue gown which emphasised her bump and her long, dark curls fell elegantly around her shoulders. She was beaming at William's very public display of affection for her.

Nina, however, was sitting quietly at a table with Daniel and the girl that he was courting, Anita Fawcett. Daniel and Anita were laughing and joking together and Nina was observing everyone and everything in the room over the rim of her wine glass which she was holding to her lips.

Stefan was sitting across the room, drinking whiskey and playing cards with some of the other men, and every so often, he would catch Nina's eye and smile, which made her stomach tingle with longing.

All of a sudden, William lifted his glass in the air and tapped a silver spoon against the glass. Immediately, the large room fell silent and everybody turned their heads towards William.

"Good evening, everyone, I hope you are enjoying the festivities," William said, addressing the room.

There were a few cheers and a short applause, and then William began again.

"It is a very exciting time for the *Shrewd Seven*. We have secured a glass crate of *very* expensive jewellery…"

There was another applause.

"And I have succeeded in bribing a few of the officers at the police station. They will now offer me information in exchange for money, which will prove very advantageous for us…"

Lolita kissed William's cheek.

"In keeping with this," William continued, his dark eyes twinkling in the chandelier light, "my new eyes and ears at the station have told me that a new Police Commissioner has been appointed. He is a young man in his twenties, and he goes by the name of James Bancroft."

Nina looked over at Stefan and she noticed that his mouth had fallen open in surprise. She tried to catch his eye, but he hurriedly closed his mouth and began staring resolutely at his glass of whiskey as though he were in deep thought.

"Do you all remember the night of the failed gun crate heist?" William asked the room.

There was a murmur of acknowledgement.

"Well, this James Bancroft was one of the officers that arrested Lucas Monroe and the others, and you will never believe what my new spies have told me…"

Everybody hung on William's words, waiting for his revelation.

"They have overheard the new Commissioner talking in the office, and it turns out that he took quite a fancy to Lolita that night."

The men in the room jeered and Lolita grinned and swept her hair away from her face.

"I think we can use this information to our advantage. What do you think, lads?" William cried, sneering and squeezing Lolita's right hip. "My suggestion is that I will strike a bargain with this James Bancroft. I will offer him one night with Lolita in exchange for the release of Lucas, Robert, Oscar and Harry. It is about time that we had our men back."

Nina raised her eyebrows. On the one hand, she was looking forward to Lucas' release, but on the other hand, she did not agree with William's methods.

"So you see, men, it is a very good time for the *Shrewd Seven* now. Peelers are just as corrupt as we are. You just need to know which buttons to press to get what you want out of them." William said, raising his glass in the air again. "Let us toast to the *Shrewd Seven*."

Everybody in the room stood and raised their glasses, and after this, the festivities continued. The men continued playing cards, and the women continued dancing. William left Lolita's side and sidled over to the table where Stefan was sitting. Nina seized this opportunity to approach her elder sister. She took hold of Lolita's arm and took her to a corner of the room where their conversation would not be overheard.

"Are you insane?" Nina hissed to Lolita. "You cannot sleep with the Police Commissioner."

"And why not?" Lolita slurred. She had clearly consumed a lot of wine.

"Well, for one thing, you are probably old enough to be his mother…" Lolita looked scorned, but Nina continued. "And for another thing, you are heavily pregnant…"

"Oh, for God's sake, Nina!" Lolita snapped. "My age and my pregnancy do not diminish my beauty! Am I not still beautiful?"

"Yes, yes, of course you are," Nina said dismissively. "But does it not bother you that William will willingly... offer... you to other men, like you are some sort of... possession of his?"

"Why would it bother me?" Lolita asked, swaying on the spot. "Men use weapons to bend other men to their will. I am using my body for the same reason. I will do whatever I need to do to ensure the survival of the *Seven*."

Nina rolled her eyes.

"I thought this is what you wanted, Nina," Lolita continued. "I thought you wanted Lucas to be released?"

"I do, but not like this!" Nina cried.

"Then please stop this," Lolita said and placed her finger to Nina's lips. Her eyes were extremely unfocused. "Anyway, is there a bowl or something near here? I feel like I might-"

Lolita did not finish her sentence. Instead, she bent forwards and vomited on the floor. Nina closed her eyes, praying for patience, and took her sister by the arm.

"Come on, I'll take you to bed, Lolita," Nina said, pulling her sister away from the vomit and summoning a servant to clean the floor.

"No! I want to dance," Lolita slurred and started to pull away from Nina.

"No, you are coming with me," Nina said sternly, and steered her sister out of the ballroom.

CHAPTER XV

June 1905

In the six weeks that had passed since Nina had cared for the inebriated Lolita, several things had happened in very quick succession. Firstly, Commissioner Bancroft had accepted William's offer, and Lolita had slept with the young man. "I liked his enthusiasm and stamina," Lolita had said crudely, to which Nina had shook her head in exasperation. And secondly, after his night with Lolita, the Commissioner had signed the release papers for Lucas and the other men. When Nina had greeted Lucas at the prison exit, he had smiled weakly, and Nina had felt that he was a mere shadow of his former self. Despite the men's release, William had ordered that the *Shrewd Seven* members remain at Sinclair Manor for the foreseeable future for their safety and protection. Apparently, in spite of their agreement, William did not trust the new Commissioner to keep the peace between them.

Nina had spent weeks caring for Lucas by day, and once he was asleep, she had been going to Stefan's bedroom at night. Nina and Stefan's relationship was stronger than ever, and they had both agreed that they would not let Lucas' presence disrupt their time together. If Nina was honest with herself, her feelings for Stefan were also stronger than ever. Although Nina pitied Lucas in his current state, she had not forgotten how he had treated her over the course of their marriage. With Lucas, she had felt neglected and unwanted, but with Stefan, she felt truly alive. Nina knew that once Lucas had recovered from his spell in prison, he would resume his affairs and his poor treatment of her.

Sure enough, on one particularly warm and sunny day in June,

Lucas had left the manor early in the morning and Nina could tell from his manner that he was going to spend time with Rosalyn Whittaker. She did not mind; in fact, it suited her. Furthermore, Lolita's estranged husband Robert, now out of prison, could not bear the sight of his heavily pregnant ex-wife, so he usually spent his days elsewhere. Today Robert had convinced some of the men (including Daniel) to accompany him to the nearby inn for a day of gambling and drinking, so the only people left at the manor were Nina, Stefan, Lolita, and William. Lolita and William usually kept to themselves upstairs so this was a perfect opportunity for Nina and Stefan to spend some time together.

They decided to go for a walk together through Sinclair Manor's grounds and then through the nearby hills and woodland areas. It had been a very pleasant day so far. They had walked hand in hand for hours, talking and laughing together. Nina had even packed a picnic so they ate a delicious lunch together on a grassy hill which overlooked the many neighbouring manors and their vast grounds.

"What do you think the future has in store for us, Nina?" Stefan asked, lying back on the grass and looking up at the clouds.

Nina's heart began to beat wildly against her chest. They did not normally discuss the future. It did not seem wise to dwell on such dreams. She lay back and rested her head on his chest.

"I don't know, Stefan, but I really hope that my future has you in it…"

"As do I," he said thoughtfully. Nina liked how his chest quivered against her cheek as he spoke.

"Wouldn't it be lovely if we could spend every day like this - just the two of us?" Stefan continued.

Nina nodded and made a noise of agreement and longing. She closed her eyes and enjoyed breathing in the scent of Stefan's skin so close to hers. She felt content and she did not want this day to end...

*

As the sky began to grow dark, Nina and Stefan decided that they had better return to the manor. As they walked back through the grass and woodland, Nina noticed that her skirts were dirty at the bottom where they had accumulated some of the leaves and mud from the ground. All too soon, the manor loomed into their view as they walked. Nina had loved being together out in the open and now, as they walked back into the manor's hallway, she knew that they would have to revert back to reality – hiding their relationship from everyone. A dark cloud of sadness enveloped her thoughts as Stefan let go of her hand and moved so that he was an appropriate distance from her. She missed his touch instantly and wished desperately that they didn't have to pretend that their relationship was platonic. Just as Nina and Stefan resolved to spend the remainder of the evening in the drawing room with some drinks, the sound of raised voices and breaking glass filled their ears. They looked at each other, startled, and walked quickly towards the dining room, which was the source of the noise. Stefan pushed open the door and Nina was shocked to see William and Lolita standing a few feet apart, both red in the face, and clearly in the middle of a ferocious argument. William's teeth were bared and Lolita's hair was standing on end as though she had run her hands through it in frustration. In his anger, William had clearly launched some glass vases against the wall, as the floor was littered with miniscule shards of glass.

"I told you to keep the jewels safe, Lolita, not to wear one as a fucking trinket!" William roared, his eyes popping wildly towards her.

"It's this baby, William, she is making me behave in strange ways. I cannot think straight!" Lolita shouted back and ran her hands through her hair in frustration.

"What is going on here?" Stefan asked. "We heard loud voices and breaking glass, so we just wanted to come and see that everything was alright…"

William and Lolita turned to look at them. Neither of them had the grace to look ashamed of themselves for the destruction of Stefan's dining room. They were both as aggressive and stubborn as each other.

"This stupid bitch decided that she would wear one of the sapphires from the jewellery raid on a chain around her neck, and she has only gone and lost it!" William cried, pointing his finger accusingly at Lolita who scowled back at him.

"It is one jewel of many, William, I'm sure that you will still make a profit from the others…" Stefan began but William interjected angrily.

"Yes, but you don't know *where* she has lost it, do you?"

"Does it matter?" Stefan asked.

"Yes, because she has admitted that the last time she remembers wearing it was the night she slept with the Commissioner. I bet that she lost it there. So now that valuable sapphire is probably in the hands of the peelers!" William snapped. "Now they will put two and two together and connect us with the jewellery theft!"

"Stop being so dramatic, William," Lolita said scathingly. "It might not be there, and anyway, if it is, I'm sure you could bribe him again to keep him on our side."

William was breathing heavily through his nose. "You shouldn't be so careless, Lolita. I thought I could trust you to keep the jewels safe. Clearly I was wrong…"

"No!" Lolita shouted. "You *can* trust me! I –"

But before Lolita could finish her sentence, she screamed and clutched her stomach, doubling over in pain. As Nina looked down, she could see that Lolita's skirts were drenched and the carpet around her was dark and damp. Clearly, it was time.

"Nina!" Lolita shrieked. "What is happening?"

Nina had never before seen her sister look so scared and vulnerable and it was unnerving.

"I think that the baby is coming, darling," Nina said slowly, walking forwards to Lolita's side.

"What?" Lolita cried. "I am not ready yet! Oh my fucking God! I knew that I didn't feel well today!"

The colour, too, had drained from William's face. He was gazing at Lolita with an expression of mingled fear and concern which was very unlike him.

"Stefan," he commanded at once.

"Yes, William?"

"Please take care of Lolita, and make sure that she delivers this baby safely. Please," William said imploringly.

Stefan nodded. Lolita let out another yell as her insides clearly convulsed with pain.

"This is all your fucking fault, William," Lolita spat. "'Don't worry, Lolita, you won't get pregnant, everything will be fine,'" she cried in a shrill, mocking voice. "Ha! That's the last time I'll ever listen to you!"

Lolita's words hung excruciatingly in the air around them. William let out a deep sigh and Nina and Stefan did not dare to react to this pivotal news. Nina did not feel as surprised as she ought to… Perhaps she had always known deep down that William had fathered the child…

"Do not breathe a word of this to anyone. If you do, the consequences will be severe," William whispered dangerously, glaring at Stefan and Nina. "Just care for her and the baby, please."

Stefan and Nina nodded again.

"Right, Lolita, come on, let's get you upstairs," Stefan said and put his arm around Lolita. Nina did the same. As they helped Lolita on her way, Nina noticed that William had poured himself a glass of brandy and had sat down at the dining table with his head in his hands.

*

A few hours had passed. Lolita was lying in bed and every so often she would scream and writhe in pain as she endured her labour contractions. Each time one passed, Nina offered her hand to Lolita to squeeze, and she was beginning to regret this decision, as her hand was now red and felt numb. Although Stefan was a highly talented and experienced doctor, Nina could tell that he was nervous about delivering the baby. He had not done this before, as of course, it was women's business, but Nina knew that he would be professional and meticulous. Lolita was truly in the best hands.

"Right, Lolita, I would like to examine you if you don't mind," Stefan said tentatively.

"Ha! You already know what is down there, and as I recall, I didn't mind so much the last time," Lolita breathed between contractions.

Nina's heart jolted. What the hell did she mean by that? Nina usually turned a deaf ear to her sister's crude remarks, but this time she could not ignore it. Nina glared at Stefan, silently demanding an answer.

Stefan raised his eyebrows. "Really, Lolita, I don't think that is appropriate..."

Nina did not avert her livid gaze and Stefan looked ashamedly at her, silently mouthing the words "I will tell you later." Nina put her hands on her hips, demanding more of an explanation, but Stefan flashed her a look which plainly said "Now is not the time to discuss this." Nina took a deep breath to steady herself. She supposed that Stefan could not be blamed for what had happened in the past, but she could not help but be incensed by the knowledge that Lolita and Stefan had - no, she couldn't even think about it.

Nina shook her head and tried to quash these thoughts and images from her mind's eye. She needed to help Lolita and the baby, after all...

*

Yet more time had passed, and Lolita's labour had continued well into the early hours of the morning. Nina was exhausted, but she knew that her exhaustion was inconsequential when compared to that of Lolita. Lolita was now crying and shrieking in pain constantly. Nina had a cold cloth pressed to her sister's forehead, and she was massaging Lolita's neck and shoulders.

"Nina, I just want this to be over. You are a stronger woman than me for enduring this. I did not hear any complaints from you when you had Daniel…" She said breathlessly.

Nina smiled. "You weren't listening properly, then. I can assure you that I cried and shouted a lot."

"Nina was also a lot younger than you are now," Stefan said matter-of-factly to Lolita. "So it may have been somewhat easier for her body to cope. Due to your age, this might be a little bit more intense for you, Lolita."

Lolita glared at Stefan, but just before she could reprimand him for his comment, another contraction passed and she shrieked with pain, hot tears spilling from her eyes.

Stefan was looking at his watch with his brow furrowed.

"Alright, Lolita, if my calculations are correct, I think that it is time…" he said.

Lolita turned to look at Nina and her eyes were wide with terror.

"I'm scared, Nina…" she whispered.

"It's alright, Lolita," Nina replied and took hold of her sister's hand and raised it to her lips. "I am with you."

*

"Alright, Lolita, I can see the head, push again please," Stefan commanded, twenty minutes later.

"If you tell me to push again, I will push my fist into your face," Lolita cried, breathing heavily. Her grip on Nina's hand was excruciating, but Nina did not complain.

"There is the Lolita we know and love," Nina chuckled, and Stefan smiled in spite of himself.

Despite her anger, Lolita gave one final push and Nina gasped as the sound of the baby's cries filled the air. Lolita sighed and relaxed. She looked exhausted. Stefan cut the umbilical cord and took the baby across the room while Nina caressed her sister's face.

"Is she alright?" Lolita called breathlessly.

"Your baby is healthy, and will be cleaned momentarily," called Stefan.

"You did it, sister," Nina said, her eyes filling with tears.

"Where is my baby?" Lolita asked, sitting up in the bed.

"Here," said Stefan softly, and he placed the baby into Lolita's waiting arms. "I have cleaned her up and covered her in a blanket. You were right, Lolita, you are now the mother of a beautiful baby girl. Congratulations."

Nina squealed with joy as she took in the image of the baby girl. She had a head of dark hair and a tiny, button nose. Lolita began to cry softly as the baby's tiny fingers curled around her own.

"She's so tiny…" Lolita gasped, looking down at her daughter. "I can't believe that I made her…"

"She's beautiful," Nina whispered and bent down to kiss the child on the forehead.

"She weighs five pounds and five ounces," Stefan said. "I suspect she has arrived a little early but she seems fine. I am sure that she will put on more weight once she starts feeding. I will go and fetch William. The placenta should be along any moment now, so prepare yourself, Lolita." Stefan smiled at the new mother and baby before he turned and left the room.

"The - what?" Lolita cried, clutching hold of Nina's hand once more.

"It's okay, it's just what happens after birth," Nina explained. " It's nothing to worry about; the placenta is what has been feeding her while she has been inside you."

Lolita looked horrified so Nina stroked her sister's hair and spoke again to distract her.

"Oh, Lolita, she is so dainty and sweet! What will you call her?"

"Karina," Lolita began. "Like the star constellation. She is my little star. I will call her Karina Belmont."

"Our maiden name?" Nina asked. "Not Rosethorn?"

"No. She is a Belmont like me," Lolita said and cradled her baby who had now fallen asleep. "She is perfect."

CHAPTER XVI

June 1905

The night had been long and emotionally draining for Nina, so she was glad to retreat to Stefan's bedroom after William had joined Lolita and Karina. As William had laid eyes on his new baby daughter, Nina had thought (or possibly imagined) that his expression had softened somewhat. It was the first time that Nina had ever seen William display a benevolent emotion. There was no sign that Lucas or Daniel or any of the other men had returned home, so Nina felt no qualms about enjoying the company of Stefan for the short remainder of the night.

Despite her exhaustion, Nina's mind was still reeling with the events of the night; so much so that she was unable to relax her thoughts and fall asleep. Stefan, after having delivered the baby, was evidently feeling the same, as after a few moments of embracing Nina under the covers, he got out of bed and began pouring two glasses of wine at the dresser at the far side of the room.

"Since we cannot sleep, we may as well have some drinks and celebrate the birth of baby Karina," Stefan said, and climbed back into bed, passing a glass to Nina, who shuffled into a sitting position against the soft pillows.

"Stefan, you were amazing tonight. Lolita was very lucky to have you there," Nina said, draining her first glass of wine quite quickly.

"Do you think so?" Stefan asked, also draining his glass. He poured more wine into their glasses as he continued. "I have only ever read about childbirth in books, so it was all new for me."

"I think you were very professional," Nina said and rested her head on his bare shoulder.

They toasted baby Karina Belmont with their wine and then continued talking and drinking until daylight streamed in through the drapes, illuminating the two empty wine bottles which adorned the bedside cabinet.

"I knew there was something else that I wanted to talk to you about!" Nina said at last. Something had been irking her, but in all the excitement of the night, she had temporarily forgotten about what Lolita had said before she had given birth.

"Oh no," Stefan said, smirking as he struggled to keep his eyes focused on her. "Am I about to be interrogated about my sexual history again?"

"Right you are, Stefan Sinclair," Nina slurred and turned so that she was facing him in bed. "What happened between you and my sister?"

Stefan smiled and caressed her cheek. "You are so inquisitive, Nina. Very well," he began. "It first happened years ago. As you know, my wife Lara died and I was therefore a very lonely young man. Lolita made herself available to me and I had no reason to refuse her offer."

Nina felt an uncomfortable pang in her stomach. She did not like the thought of Stefan with Lolita, but again, she reminded herself that she could not be annoyed about something that had happened long before they had commenced their relationship.

"So did it just happen once?" Nina asked, closing her eyes in the hope that a lack of vision would stop the spinning sensation that she was experiencing.

"Erm, no. Quite a few times over the years, actually," Stefan said sheepishly.

Nina sighed.

"You wanted to know the truth, Nina, so there you have it," Stefan continued. "I can assure you that those encounters meant nothing to me, and I know that they certainly meant nothing to Lolita. Please don't be upset by a few insignificant romps that I would rather forget about."

Nina opened her eyes again, but alas, she still felt like the room was spinning around her. "When was the last time?"

"About two or three years ago, maybe?" Stefan said. "I'm not proud of it, especially not now. I would never have dreamed that I would be lucky enough to be with you. If I had thought there was even a chance that you and I could be together I wouldn't have gone anywhere near her. I wish I could undo the past, but I can't."

"Why didn't you tell me this?" Nina asked.

"Oh, come on, Nina," Stefan laughed. "Is there ever a good time to admit that you have slept with the sister of the woman that you – "

He stopped in his tracks and frowned to himself. He seemed to have been on the verge of divulging something, but had caught himself just in time.

"The woman that you – what?" Nina asked, pushing his chest flirtatiously, attempting to coax the unbidden words from his lips. Her heart was beating wildly against her chest and her breath became caught in her throat.

He smirked again and gazed deeply into her eyes. Before he spoke, he twirled a strand of her hair around his finger.

"Alright... the woman that you *love*," Stefan said with an air of finality, and smiled an irresistible smile.

Nina gasped and gazed back into his round, dark eyes. She saw her own flushed yet elated face reflected there.

"You love me?" she whispered disbelievingly.

"Yes, Nina, I love you..." Stefan whispered, and gently gripped her waist with his hands. He guided her body towards him so that she was sitting astride him on the bed.

Nina pushed her blonde, wavy hair behind her ears, and leant forwards towards him. Before their lips met, she whispered: "I love you, too…"

Nina kissed Stefan's lips passionately and ran her hands through his sleek, dark hair. She tried not to think of the implications that their newly disclosed feelings would have on their secret, forbidden affair.

Their lips parted, and Stefan began kissing her neck and caressing her breasts with his soft hands.

"Nina, when I delivered that baby tonight, I realised something."

"What?" Nina asked and moved her body down on top of Stefan so that she could kiss his stomach.

"I am forty years old, and I have never had a child," Stefan continued, slurring his words and closing his eyes.

Nina began kissing Stefan's inner thighs. He sighed and held the top of her head with his hands.

"I want to be a father," he said breathlessly as Nina explored his lower body with her mouth and tongue.

"Stefan Sinclair, you are drunk," Nina said after a few moments. She moved herself back up so that her face was level with his and placed her legs either side of his hips.

"Yes I am, but I mean it, Nina, I want everything with you…"

"Alright, Stefan, I will believe you when you are sober," Nina smirked and brought her body down on top of his. She gripped his shoulders as pangs of pleasure soared around her body like wildfire. He kissed her lips hungrily and caressed her hips as she moved on top of him.

"I love you, Nina, I love you so much… I don't ever want to be apart from you…" he whispered into her ear.

Nina smiled and held his head close to hers as they kissed and moved against each other. She doubted that she had ever before experienced this level of joy and happiness. She tried not to think about how, in a few hours, Lucas would return home, and she would have to play the part of his doting wife... The very thought made her feel nauseous...

CHAPTER XVII

June 1905

The wind had howled through the trees and the rain had clattered against the window panes of Sinclair Manor for the remainder of June. With each passing day, Lucas had showered Nina with more and more affection and attention, which unfortunately had had a diminishing effect on the amount of time that Stefan and Nina could spend together. Despite the hopeless longing that Nina felt for Stefan, she was at least happy to see that motherhood had changed Lolita for the better. Lolita absolutely doted over baby Karina, and Nina was surprised that her sister was displaying such care and patience for the child. William, too, seemed to adore his daughter, and the sight of him cooing and fussing over Karina was unsettling for Nina, who, of course, knew William to be a callous and cruel man.

All too soon, the last day of the month was upon them, and Nina awoke to Lucas' husky voice in her ear.

"Happy birthday, beautiful," he crooned and kissed her cheek.

Nina groaned. Another birthday meant that she was another year older. In Nina's mind, thirty-eight seemed much older than thirty-seven.

"Thank you, darling. Please don't make a fuss over me today, Lucas. Let's just acknowledge my getting older and get on with our day as normal…"

"Nonsense!" Lucas said with a hearty laugh. "We are having a party for you later complete with presents and dancing. I know I haven't treated you very well recently, so I want to show everyone how much I love you."

Nina's heart sank to her stomach. She wondered what Stefan

would think of Lucas' pompous display of love.

"Oh, Lucas, you shouldn't have..." Nina began awkwardly.

"Don't worry, Nina, it will be a nice evening, and then perhaps when we go to bed, I can show you how much you mean to me."

Nina winced as though he had doused her with cold water. She had not been intimate with Lucas since he had returned from prison, and she had no immediate plans to do so. She had not forgotten his frequent visits to Rosalyn, nor did she want to be unfaithful to Stefan.

*

True to his word, Lucas had organised a truly extravagant birthday party for Nina. The ballroom of Sinclair Manor was adorned with flowers and the servants were carrying golden trays laden with glasses of red wine, which was Nina's favourite beverage. By the ballroom's ornate, golden double doors stood a large rectangular table where the *Seven*'s members had placed gifts for Nina. Nina could not help but feel immensely grateful for the amount of gifts she had received, for the families had been very generous.

After a couple of hours of drinking and dancing, Lucas announced to the room that Nina was going to open some of her presents from her immediate family and friends. Not liking to be the centre of attention, Nina had politely suggested to Lucas that she would open her presents upstairs but he did not seem to take her seriously. All of the *Seven* members and their families crowded around the round table where Nina, Lucas, Daniel, Stefan, William, Lolita, and Karina were sitting.

"I want everyone to see how much I love you, Nina, so open your present from me first," Lucas slurred arrogantly.

Nina took a deep breath and her eyes rested on Stefan who was sitting directly opposite her at the table. He caught her eye for a fraction of a second before averting his gaze. Nina's eyes roved around the room and she could feel the colour rising in her cheeks as she saw a multitude of faces all focused on her. Rosalyn Whittaker was standing in the crowd around the table. Her eyes were narrowed and her lips were pursed as though she was sucking on a particularly bitter lemon.

Nina unwrapped Lucas' gift to reveal a rectangular velvet box. She opened the box and upon the red satin material lay a gold necklace. At the bottom of the beautiful chain there was a large, round ruby which glittered in the lamplight. Nina gasped at the beauty of the necklace and thanked Lucas profusely. He beamed and kissed her on the lips, before placing the necklace around her pale neck. As he did so, Nina looked across the table to see Stefan draining a glass of red wine in one. Her insides writhed at the thought of upsetting Stefan, but there was nothing she could do about it at the moment. Her thoughts wandered to the next time she and Stefan could be together. She would make up for this charade then.

Over the next half an hour, Nina was presented with gift after gift, and her face was aching from all of the smiling she had been forced to do. Lolita had given her a bottle of her favourite perfume, Daniel had given her the earrings to match the ruby necklace, and the other guests had spoiled her with flowers and wine and chocolates. At last, the pile of gifts had dwindled, and there was one last gift to open.

"Ah, yes, that gift is from me," said Stefan nonchalantly, clearing his throat and addressing Nina as though she were a mere family friend.

Nina's heart leapt. This was the gift that she had been waiting for. With hands shaking eagerly, she ripped open the wrapping paper to reveal a thick, brown, leather-bound book. In gold letters on the front cover read the words: *The Complete Works of William Shakespeare*. Nina felt a twinge beneath her nose and she felt her eyes filling with tears, but she blinked them away furiously.

"Thank you, Stefan, you know how much I love Shakespeare's

plays," Nina said quietly.

"You're welcome, Nina," Stefan said, not quite meeting her gaze. "Shakespeare is a shared interest that Nina and I have, you see," he said to the crowd.

"Yes, yes, very well," Lucas said pompously. "Now that Nina has finished opening her gifts, we can all go back to drinking and dancing. Thank you everyone for your kind words and gifts. I am very grateful to everyone for making Nina's birthday very special."

"Yes, thank you, everyone," Nina said, and after a toast to Nina's good health, the crowd dispersed. The string quartet resumed the playing of their instruments and Nina reached for the nearest glass of wine with her right hand. Her left hand was still clutching the leather book and she was surreptitiously holding it close to her chest.

*

As the oil lamps dimmed in the ballroom, the *Shrewd Seven* members and their families started to vacate the ballroom and ascend the staircase in search of their beds.

Lucas had not left Nina's side all night, and as he walked away to ask the servants to tidy up, Stefan seemed to seize the opportunity to talk to Nina alone. He took her hand in his and raised it to his lips, but his eyes were fixed on Lucas, obviously ensuring that Lucas was out of earshot.

"I hope that you like the book," Stefan whispered, now looking into her eyes.

"Oh, Stefan, I love it…" Nina began.

"Turn to the back of the book, and you will notice that there is a slit in the leather. Inside this you will find a letter from me," he said, now whispering quickly as Lucas began walking towards them.

"Alright, thank you, Stefan," Nina said quietly and let go of his hand as Lucas reached her side and put his arm around her waist.

"Are you ready for bed, darling?" Lucas said and kissed her cheek.

"Yes, I think so," Nina said. "Goodnight, Stefan."

Stefan nodded cordially, but there was a sadness behind his eyes that only Nina could recognise.

"Alright. Goodnight, Stefan," Lucas said and with that, he took Nina's hand and led her out of the room. Nina turned her head back to look at Stefan and he gave her a sort of half-smile which told her that he wished that he could be the one that was leading her upstairs to bed.

*

Luckily for Nina, Lucas had been too drunk to beg her for intimacy when they reached their bedroom. As soon as he had got into bed, he had fallen asleep. Now Nina was left alone with only the sound of his snores for company, and she thought that now was the perfect time to look at the book that Stefan had given to her. She walked across the room to the dressing table and sat down with the book in her hands. Her fingers trembled as she flicked to the back of the book. She could see the neat little slit in the leather that Stefan had described. It was very subtle, and she doubted that anyone would notice it if they had not been looking for it. She slid her fingers inside the material and retrieved a little slip of parchment from inside the secret compartment. Her breath hitched in her throat as she unfolded the parchment, and her eyes devoured the words hungrily as she took in Stefan's sophisticated, cursive handwriting:

Dearest Nina,

Happy birthday, darling. I thought that you would like this book as I know how much you like the work of Shakespeare. I also thought that this book could help us to convey messages to each other without arousing any suspicion amongst our friends and acquaintances. I wish that I could give you something more exquisite and expen-

sive than this book, but doing so would definitely raise questions. So instead, I settled for this unobtrusive gift. I hope that we can be together again soon, Nina. It is very hard for me to watch you with Lucas, especially now that he has decided that he adores you again. I know that it isn't your fault. I just wish that there was a way that we could openly be together without the worry of being disowned or worse. By the time you are reading this, it will probably be night time, so I hope that you have had a lovely birthday. I know that you have been worrying about getting older, but please do not fret, because to me, you are perfect in every way. I love you, Nina. I love you more every time that I see you.

All my love, always,

S

Two large tears rolled down her cheeks as she finished reading. She held the parchment to her heart and sobbed quietly in front of the mirror...

CHAPTER XVIII

August 1905

A persistent feeling of tenderness and nausea, a heightened sensitivity to smells, the agonising absence of a monthly cycle... Nina had experienced these symptoms once before, but to have them now, given her affair with Stefan, was deeply disconcerting for Nina. *Surely not,* Nina told herself, *I absolutely cannot be* – Nina halted her own thoughts. She would not even allow herself to consider the possibility. Instead, she cast her mind back to a conversation she had once had with her mother when she was alive. Her mother had told her that there comes a time in a woman's life when her monthly cycles and thus her reproductive capabilities cease. *Yes*, Nina thought, *that is what is happening. It must be* –

"Mrs Monroe, step this way please," a voice called, shattering Nina's frenzied reverie. Nina looked up to see a fair-haired man in a tweed jacket standing in the doorway in front of her. Normally, Nina would not visit a physician's office - she would ask Stefan to examine and treat her - but of course, this time it would be inappropriate for him to do so. Nina took a deep breath, stood up, and walked into the room with the air of someone who was resigned to the gallows...

*

Later that afternoon, Nina and Lolita were sitting together in the drawing room of Sinclair Manor. Nina was cradling baby Karina in her arms and looking down at the child's sweet, innocent face. Her eyes were dark like her mother's and the longer Nina looked at Karina, the more Nina felt at ease with what the physician had told her earlier in the day. *No,* Nina thought, scolding herself, *I will not think about this until I have told Stefan.*

Lolita was fawning over herself in the mirror in the corner of the room. Though her face was bare and paler than normal due to a lack of makeup, Lolita was still truly beautiful. Her dark curls were pinned to her head and pulled into an elegant bun on top of her head, and the grey corset that she wore beneath her dress complemented her curvaceous figure - she had already lost the majority of her pregnancy weight around her midsection. She ran her hands down over her stomach and surveyed her reflection with a frown and a pout.

"Has Karina ruined my body, Nina?" Lolita asked, turning around to face Nina with her hands on her hips.

"Certainly not," Nina replied absently, still looking down at the smiling baby in her arms. "You look much better than all the new mothers that I have ever seen."

Lolita sighed and walked over to Nina. Nina passed Karina to her mother and smiled as Lolita stroked the child's face.

"Well nevertheless, you are worth it all, Karina," Lolita said softly and placed a kiss on the baby's cheek.

"Were you worried, when you found out you were pregnant?" Nina whispered to Lolita.

Lolita placed Karina in her cradle and then walked back towards Nina. The two sisters sat down on the settee and raised their glasses of wine to their lips.

"I suppose so, at first," Lolita said. "Well, you know me, I never thought that I would make a good mother... Why do you ask?"

Nina felt a pang in her stomach. *Why did I ask?* She thought frantically.

"I am just curious," Nina said after a pause. "Did you know that Robert would leave you when he found out?" All of the thoughts that had been whirling around her mind since her visit to the physician now seemed to be pouring out of her mouth.

Lolita raised an eyebrow. "Well, yes, I thought that he might, but I didn't care, Nina."

"Oh? Why was that?" Nina asked, hanging on her sister's every word.

"Because I knew that the baby was William's, and I knew that I loved William. You know I only married Robert because mother and father had arranged it. I never loved him, and he never loved me, so it was no great loss, really." Lolita said absent-mindedly, examining the fingernails on her right hand.

Nina lifted her hand to her mouth and began tracing a finger around her lips. She became immersed in her own thoughts as Lolita poured another glass of wine for them. Was her situation that different to Lolita's, really? What was going to happen to her?

Suddenly, Karina's high-pitched cries pierced the air and as Lolita stood to fuss over the child, Nina seized the Shakespeare book that Stefan had given to her, a quill and piece of parchment from the nearby table and wrote a note to Stefan as quickly as she could.

We need to talk. Not at the Manor. I will meet you in your office at the hospital in an hour. Yours, always, Nina.

With trembling hands, Nina folded the parchment and slid it into the hidden compartment at the back of the book. She excused herself from her sister and quitted the room. Thankfully, her maid Lottie was polishing the furniture in the hallway. Nina walked over and passed the book to the young girl.

"Take this book to Dr Sinclair please," Nina said. "He is at the nearby inn *The Raven* with the other men."

"Yes, Mistress Monroe," Lottie said. She curtsied and immediately left to retrieve her coat.

*

One hour later, Nina had arrived at the hospital and had taken a seat in the wooden chair at Stefan's desk. His office was a small room with wood-panelled walls and a small fireplace. A large bookcase stood at the back of the room. Its shelves were laden with all sorts of medical journals and prestigious looking books. On the wall behind Stefan's desk were all sorts of framed certificates that he had earned. Just as Nina began to read one of them, the door opened and she turned in her seat to see Stefan in the doorway. He looked as handsome as ever, with his windswept hair and shirt unbuttoned at the neck. Stefan knelt down in front of Nina who was still sitting in the chair and he placed a kiss on her lips.

"Are you alright, Nina, darling? You said that we needed to talk…" he began.

"We do, Stefan," Nina said, looking into his dark, penetrating eyes, and caressing his stubbly cheek with her right hand.

"Is everything alright?" Stefan continued, now placing Nina's other hand in his own and raising it to his lips.

"It depends how you feel about this…" Nina began, taking a deep breath to steady herself.

Stefan said nothing but continued to gaze imploringly into her eyes.

"I am pregnant," she said at last. "I visited a physician this morning and he confirmed it. It is your baby, Stefan. I haven't been intimate with Lucas for a while."

There was a slight pause. Nina could feel her heart beating rapidly against her chest. She could practically hear Stefan's mind whirring as he processed her words. To her intense relief, his face broke into a wide smile.

"Nina, this is wonderful!" he cried and placed a hand on her stomach. "I told you that I want everything with you, Nina, I really do."

He took both of her hands in his own and guided her into a standing position. He cupped his hands around her neck and kissed her lips passionately.

Nina pulled her face away from his. "Do you mean it, Stefan? What are we going to do about Lucas?"

"Nina, don't worry about that now, we will work everything out in time. I am so happy," Stefan said, smiling at her and pulling her close to him once more.

Nina felt herself becoming lost in the moment with Stefan, as she so often did. Yes, there was no need to worry about the formalities now. They could just celebrate this joyful news together, here and now…

Stefan lifted Nina by the waist and placed her so that she was sitting on the edge of his desk. He kissed her cheek and neck and his hands began clawing at the laces of her corset around her bust. Nina melted at his touch and closed her eyes, ready as ever to feel his lips on her bare chest and more. Until…

"What the fuck?"

Nina and Stefan froze. In the heat of the moment, they had not heard the office door open behind them. They had not heard the sobbing baby, but they had heard the stern, shocked voice of Lolita…

Stefan jumped away from Nina as though she had burned him, and Nina hastily hoisted the material of her dress over her breasts.

"Lolita…" Nina began. Her heart had plummeted into her stomach and her breath hitched in her throat. This could not be happening…

Lolita merely stood framed in the doorway, aghast at what she had seen. Her lips were parted and her eyes were wide with shock. She did not appear to hear Karina who was still wailing in her arms.

Words had utterly failed Nina. What was her sister going to do with this information?

CHAPTER XIX

August 1905

Only the high-pitched wails of Karina permeated the thick atmosphere between Stefan and the two sisters. After a few excruciating moments of stunned stupor, Lolita's initial shock at the discovery of her youngest sister and one of her many ex-lovers had clearly subsided because her scarlet painted lips curved into an amused smirk.

"Well, well, well, baby sister, I never would have dreamed that you had it in you," Lolita said, her eyes dancing gleefully between Stefan and Nina.

"I..." Nina started awkwardly, but Lolita interjected.

"I never thought that you would give Lucas a taste of his own medicine, but Jesus Christ, you fooled me!" she cried with a scornful laugh.

Nina glanced sideways at Stefan, who rolled his eyes back at her.

"He's a great lover, isn't he, sister?" Lolita continued, sneering at the exasperated expression on Stefan's face and gently rocking Karina in her arms as the child continued to cry.

"Lolita!" Nina snapped hotly, glaring at her sister. Lolita was quite clearly taking great pleasure in taunting them.

"Oh, it's alright, I'm not going to steal him from you. Although being in this office does bring back some good memories..." Lolita drawled, her dark eyes lingering on the large wooden desk and a knowing smirk playing around her lips. Nina's mouth fell open but before she could retort, Lolita cut across her, her eyes practically twinkling with jubilance. "Oh, cheer up, I'm proud of you, Nina. I never liked Lucas and I always thought that you could do better than him. And now you have!"

Stefan was staring at Lolita as though he would like nothing more than for her to stop talking.

"Is there a reason for your intrusion?" he asked quietly through gritted teeth.

"As a matter of fact, yes," Lolita began waspishly. "But we are in no way finished discussing this…" She pointed her finger playfully between them before continuing. "As you can hear, my darling daughter will not stop crying, and I believe that she might be unwell. I went to find you at the inn but the men said that you had left to attend to an emergency at the hospital," Her lip curled into another jeering smile. "Nevertheless, now that I have found you, please can you examine her and check that she is alright? I don't know how much more of this wailing I can take…"

Stefan walked forwards and took the baby from her mother's arms. He looked down at the child's anguished features and murmured "I will need to go and fetch my thermometer," before quitting the room, leaving Nina alone with Lolita.

Nina braced herself for the interrogation that was surely on its way.

"So?" Lolita asked, walking towards Nina with her hands on her hips. Her eyes were still twinkling with amusement. "How long has this been going on, then?"

Nina knew that her sister positively revelled in any kind of scandal, so she sighed before she spoke.

"A while, but you cannot tell anyone, Lolita. Promise that you won't."

Lolita laughed scornfully. "Ha! Oh come on, Nina, I know how this works. I will not tell anyone."

Nina looked into Lolita's eyes. In truth, she trusted that her sister would keep the information to herself. A part of Nina wanted Lolita to know that her relationship with Stefan was serious, lest her sister would try and sink her claws into him again.

"Alright," Nina began. "We have been together since January…"

"Wow!" Lolita cried. "Nina, you dark horse, I never would have guessed! And I am usually so perceptive…" She pouted like a small child would do.

"This isn't some sordid little affair like the kind that you enjoy, you know," Nina continued sternly. "I love him and he loves me…"

Lolita had the grace to look politely stunned for a moment.

"Oh, really? That's interesting."

"Yes, really," Nina replied quietly.

"Then, what are you going to –" Lolita's question was interrupted by the sudden reappearance of Stefan and by the continued shrieking cries of her daughter.

"Oh God, she's back…" Lolita muttered.

"Her temperature is very high and her breathing is shallow and strained. I recommend this medicine," Stefan said, holding up a small bottle for them to see. "Two drops under her tongue three times a day, like so…" He gently opened Karina's mouth and squeezed the top of the bottle's stopper until two drops fell into the child's mouth. As the drops touched her tongue, Karina's cries came to an astonished halt.

"Have I gone deaf?" Lolita asked, clutching her ears and looking around in feigned horror.

"She has stopped crying for now," Stefan smiled. "Yes, so after a day or so she will be fine."

"Thank you, Stefan," Lolita said as he placed her daughter back into her arms. "I shall see you two lovebirds later, and don't worry…your secret's safe with me." She winked at Stefan and made for the door. As the door closed behind her, Nina and Stefan let out a collective sigh of both relief and exasperation.

Stefan walked over to Nina and held her in his arms. He kissed her forehead and Nina closed her eyes as she felt the whiskery beard and the soft lips on her skin.

"I suppose that she bombarded you with questions the moment I left the room?" Stefan asked softly.

"Naturally," Nina began. "I told her that we have been together since January and that we are serious about each other."

Stefan nodded. "And did you tell her about – "

Nina lifted her head up and pressed a finger to Stefan's lips.

"Check the door," she whispered.

"What?" Stefan asked, utterly nonplussed.

"I know my sister, and I guarantee that she will be listening intently behind the door…" Nina said, still whispering.

"No, really?" Stefan said, an amused smirk appearing around his lips.

"I'm afraid so,"

"Is she really that impertinent?" Stefan whispered back.

"Absolutely," Nina said.

With that, Stefan walked over to the door, pulled down the handle and pushed it open. Sure enough, Lolita was standing there and had quite clearly been eavesdropping.

She looked at Stefan unabashedly. "Tell me about what?" she demanded.

"Goodbye, Lolita," Nina called from the room. Lolita scowled and turned on her heel, leaving them alone at last.

Stefan closed the door behind her once more, and once again held Nina in his arms.

"It is honestly a wonder that she did not find out about us before now," Nina said, resting her head on his chest. "She is ten times more inquisitive than I am…"

Stefan smiled and began kissing her cheek again.

"Now…where were we?" he whispered into her ear.

CHAPTER XX

September 1905

The once pristine pages of *The Complete Works of William Shakespeare* were becoming furled and unkempt due to the many times that Nina's and Stefan's fingers had rifled through them. With Lolita now aware of their affair, Nina and Stefan were now apprehensive about meeting at the Manor, and so they had taken to writing almost daily letters to one another and concealing them within the leather of the book. Each time that the book fell into Nina's possession, she had retreated to her bedroom and allowed her eyes to devour the parchment, becoming truly lost in Stefan's charming words.

Early one September morning, Nina awoke to find her bedroom bathed in rich autumn sunlight. She could hear birds singing in the trees outside the window, and as she stirred and hoisted herself up into a seated position against the pillows, she became distinctly aware of the fact that she was alone in the bed. She let out a sigh of relief. Over the past few weeks, Lucas had been spending more and more time away from Sinclair Manor – he was presumably with Rosalyn Whittaker or some other woman – and therefore Nina had not had to endure his arduous attempts at seduction. He had obviously grown tired of Nina's reluctance to be intimate with him and was thankfully seeking attention elsewhere.

Nina leaned towards her bedside table and withdrew *The Complete Works of William Shakespeare* from the drawer. One of the servants had delivered the book to Nina the previous night, but she had been fearful that Lucas would come to bed so she had not dared to read the letter that was waiting for her within the book's back cover. Now, however, it was the perfect time to gaze upon her lover's sloping, cursive handwriting...

Dear Nina,

Have you had any more thoughts about the name of our child? I thought perhaps Juliet Sinclair for a girl, because we saw 'Romeo and Juliet' together at the beginning of our relationship? As for a boy's name, I have no idea, and I thought that you could...

Nina's eyes tore away from the parchment as her bedroom door swung open with such force that it hit the neighbouring wall with a resounding crash. Nina jumped and hastily tucked the letter back inside the leather of the book as her elder sister ran into the room. Lolita's eyes were bloodshot and were darting from one corner of the room to the other. Her face was tear-stained and she appeared to be shaking as she let out a frenzied shriek.

"Karina is missing!"

The words took a while to register with Nina. She merely sat staring at her distraught sister with her mouth open, while her insides seemed to become paralysed with shock. There had to be a reasonable explanation...

"Lolita, calm down," Nina began. "Are you sure that one of the servants hasn't gone to bathe her or...?"

"Of course I am sure!" Lolita snapped. "When I woke up this morning, Karina was missing from her bassinet. William and I have already spoken to all of the servants and we have searched all over the Manor. This is the last place that we have looked!"

Lolita began pacing tensely and wringing her hands as William stepped into the room. His brow was furrowed and there was a most unfamiliar expression upon his face. It was one of anguished concern.

"So she isn't in here?" he asked quietly.

"No, she isn't here or anywhere, William!" Lolita wailed, tears falling from her red eyes. "What are we going to do?"

*

Half an hour later, all of the *Seven's* members had congregated in the drawing room and there was still no sign of the missing baby. In her desperation to find her daughter, Lolita had suggested that they contact the police, but this had been met with scorn and disdain by William since the *Seven's* relationship with the police was strained to say the least.

"Come on, William," Lolita moaned. "I can get the Commissioner to help us. Perhaps I can *persuade* him…"

Nina squeezed her sister's hand sympathetically.

"I don't think so…" said Lucas, who had just re-entered the room after speaking with the servants. Everybody turned to look at Lucas. He was clutching a piece of parchment in his trembling right hand.

"One of the servants found this letter in the letterbox…" Lucas began and handed the parchment to William. "It is not good news, I am afraid…"

William's eyes roved over the parchment and his eyes narrowed with every word that he read. The room was silent. Nobody dared to ask William what was written in the letter. At last, he crumpled the parchment in his fist and threw it across the room in temper.

"What – what is it?" Lolita asked tentatively.

"That fucking bastard, Bancroft!" William exploded and punched the nearby wall, leaving a dent in the plaster. Nina looked across the room at Stefan, whose expression was sombre as he let out a sigh. The atmosphere in the room was so tense and thick that Nina felt as though her breath was being constricted and that the walls were closing in on her. Everyone seemed to shuffle awkwardly on the spot.

"What are we going to do?" Lucas asked sternly. He was standing next to William across the room from Nina. Rosalyn Whittaker was at his other side, twirling her hair around her fingers absently. Lucas had not even acknowledged Nina's presence in the room, but if she was honest, Nina couldn't care less. She was too worried about her niece's whereabouts and safety to care about marital politics at the moment.

"Whatever it takes," William said through gritted teeth. "Bancroft has found the missing sapphire that *you* lost, Lolita."

Lolita's eyes widened with shock.

"He has?" she mumbled.

"Oh yes," William continued, pointing a threatening finger at Lolita. "Do you remember it? The jewel that I asked you to keep safe? It was one of the jewels from our jewellery shop robbery? Do you remember?" His voice was getting progressively louder and more frightening with every word.

Lolita's bottom lip trembled and Nina squeezed her hand again.

"Yes, I remember," Lolita said timidly, looking at the floor. Nina had never seen her sister behave so submissively.

"Well, he has found it at his house and he has put two and two together," William said scathingly. "He has now connected us with the robbery, which of course they have been investigating."

Lolita said nothing and closed her eyes. Two tears seeped from beneath her eyelids and clung onto her eyelashes before cascading down her cheeks. All of the people in the room too remained silent, hanging on William's every word.

"Bancroft's family had recently taken ownership of the jewellery shop, would you fucking believe, so Bancroft has taken the robbery as a personal attack and has taken our daughter as ransom. He says he will return Karina to us as soon as we return all of the stolen jewels to them. Those bastards of mine on Fleet Street will need to pay for not doing their research properly, too!" William balled both of his hands into fists again and Nina was sure that she could hear his knuckles crack in the deathly silence of the room. As Nina looked around the room, she noticed that Stefan's face had turned pale and he had a nauseated expression on his face. He traced his bottom lip with his index finger before his eyes fell on Nina. He gave her a weak smile before looking away again.

"I'm – I'm sorry, William..." Lolita sobbed, falling to her knees before him.

"The fact that you are sorry does not alter the fact that he has taken our daughter!" William bellowed, seizing a glass vase from the nearby sideboard and launching it across the room where it shattered against one of the walls. The *Seven* members jumped and squealed as they shielded themselves from the flying shards of glass.

"I will find James Bancroft and I will kill him!" William roared. "Mark my words, he is a fucking dead man."

Nina gulped. Of course she knew what a dangerous man William was, but she had never before seen such malice and anger in his eyes...

CHAPTER XXI

September 1905

Dear Stefan,

With each passing day, our child grows bigger and stronger, and I cannot help but feel guilty that we have not secured his or her future yet. It is an uncertain one, with Lucas still unaware of our relationship and of our child's existence. I want nothing more than to run away with you and start our life anew somewhere else. What are we going to do, Stefan? I cannot bear not knowing when all I want to do is be with you always.

All my love,

Nina

Nina folded her letter and tucked it safely within the leather sleeve of the Shakespeare book. She opened the bedroom door quietly so as not to wake Lucas, who had graced her with his presence the previous night and was still sleeping and breathing heavily in the bed. Nina traversed the grand upstairs corridors with their wood-panelled walls and gazed idly at the exquisite painted portraits and landscapes that hung in their ornate gilded frames as she passed. At last, Nina reached Stefan's door and she slid the book underneath before walking away to find her sister who would undoubtedly be drinking wine in the drawing room downstairs.

*

As one would expect, Lolita was not coping very well with the knowledge that the Police Commissioner had taken her baby daughter. Her relationship with William was also strained due to the fact that she was partly to blame for the Commissioner's actions. As for William, he seemed entirely focused on revenge and Nina had learned from both Lucas and Stefan that William was planning to meet, or rather, ambush Bancroft at an abandoned warehouse in Lambeth two days from now.

As Nina descended the stairs, the view of Lolita sprawled on one of the settees in the hallway came into clear focus. Her shaking hands were reaching for a glass of wine on the nearby glass table. This was clearly not her first glass, Nina thought as she reached her inebriated sister.

"Lolita, it is eleven o'clock in the morning, how long have you been drinking?" Nina asked softly, sitting down beside her sister and stroking her hair.

"How long is a piece of string, Nina?" Lolita said, smirking. She sat up and drained the glass of wine in one. She was looking very dishevelled with her dark curls standing on end, her makeup smudged around her eyes and her dress creased within an inch of its life. Nina wondered if Lolita had been here all night.

"Come on now, sister, this is not going to get Karina back, is it?" Nina said, motioning to a servant to come and remove the bottle of wine.

"William will sort it out," Lolita said, slurring her words and leaning on Nina's shoulder. "He has a plan, you know. He is going to kill that peeler bastard, and bring my darling girl back to me."

Nina put her arm around her sister. Before she could offer any words of condolence, however, the front doors of Sinclair Manor swung open to reveal a figure all too familiar to Nina. The woman's flaming red hair shone in the sunlight and the skirts of her grey dress swished as she strode into the hallway.

The doorman bowed to the woman. "Miss Rosalyn Whittaker," he mumbled as she passed him.

Rosalyn's dark, heavily-lidded eyes fell on Nina and Lolita and she smirked at the sight of Lolita slumped against her sister. She stood before them with her hands on her hips and Nina felt a twinge of anger rise deep within. Who did this woman think she was?

"Lolita, you look dreadful. More so than usual, at least," Rosalyn drawled, looking down her nose at her.

"Yes, well fortunately for me, this is something a little makeup and a hairbrush can fix. You always look dreadful even when you are trying," Lolita said, sitting up and scowling at Rosalyn.

Rosalyn's lips curved into an arrogant sneer, but before she could retort, Lolita cut across her.

"What are you even doing here? Waiting for Lucas like the obedient little dog that you are?"

Rosalyn raised her eyebrows. "Well, yes, I have come to see Lucas, if you must know. But since you are so inquisitive, I would be glad to share my happy news with you... And especially with *her*..." Rosalyn added with relish, resting her gaze upon Nina who glared determinedly back at her.

Nina's palms began to grow clammy so she twisted them together in her lap before Rosalyn spoke again. Lolita stood up and walked towards Rosalyn, so that their noses were mere inches apart.

"I think that you should watch your tone when you are talking about my sister," Lolita said darkly.

"I will speak about her however I like," Rosalyn breathed back.

"Oh, really?" Lolita said, resting her hand on the sideboard to support herself, as she was swaying precariously on the spot.

"I am pregnant with Lucas' child," Rosalyn said loudly, so that Nina could hear.

The words hung in the air above them for a few moments. Nina' stomach jolted uncomfortably and her mind began formulating all sorts of plans and scenarios at rapid speed.

"Is that it?" Lolita laughed scornfully. "Is that why you are acting so arrogantly? I can assure you, *sweetheart*, that you mean nothing to Lucas, and neither will this brat you are carrying. I wouldn't be surprised if he tells you to dispose of it immediately."

"Oh, I disagree," Rosalyn said softly, smiling sarcastically and tilting her head to consider Lolita. "Lucas told me a while ago that he wants to leave Nina, that he finds her cold and boring, and that he loves me."

Nina closed her eyes and took a deep breath, hoping to quell some of the fury that was now building inside of her.

"Is that what he told you?" Lolita jeered scathingly in a voice barely more than a whisper. "You are young and still have an awful lot to learn about men. They will say anything to get what they want out of you."

Nina stood and took her place at her sister's side, looking disdainfully at Rosalyn whose eyes were twinkling with malice.

"That's enough, Lolita," Nina said. "I will remember your comments, Rosalyn, the very next time Lucas begs me to sleep with him, as he does every night."

Nina did not know why she was encouraging Rosalyn by responding to her insults, but the words seemed to tumble out of her mouth against her will.

"Like my sister has said, I doubt very much that my husband will care about the baby that you are carrying, so I think that you should leave now with your dignity, before you get your heart broken," Nina said, weighing every word.

"Now, now, ladies, what is going on?" said Lucas' voice behind them. Nina turned to look at her husband who was walking towards them slowly.

Rosalyn walked over to Lucas and took both of his hands in hers. "I am pregnant with your child, Lucas, and Nina can't accept that you love me."

Lucas' frowned at Rosalyn, looking down at her midsection with an unreadable expression.

"Isn't this wonderful, Lucas?" Rosalyn exclaimed, raising one of his hands to her lips and gazing imploringly at him. "Now you can leave Nina and we can be together…"

Lucas released Rosalyn's hand and stepped away from her.

"I don't think so," Lucas said at last, now looking deeply into Nina's eyes.

There was a very uncomfortable silence.

"What?" Rosalyn said, her voice breaking as tears threatened to fall from her eyes.

"Ha!" Lolita laughed, her eyes popping wildly. "I told you that you mean nothing to him!"

"Lolita, for once in your life, shut your fucking mouth," Lucas growled. "I will speak to you later about this, Rosalyn. I would like to speak privately with my wife now."

Rosalyn clapped a hand to her forehead and stepped backwards in disbelief.

"But," she moaned, biting her bottom lip. "What about all of the things that you said?"

Nina had both seen and heard enough. Emotions soared around her body like wildfire and all she wanted to do was flee the situation. As though driven by a motor, Nina turned and began to run. Her boots clattered loudly on the marble steps as she ran. Lucas' frenzied shouts of "Nina! Nina!" rang in her ears until she had reached the peaceful sanctuary of her bedroom. She closed the door behind her and leant against the wood. She began to cry and she felt herself sliding downwards until she had curled herself into a ball on the floor.

CHAPTER XXII

September 1905

"Nina, darling, please open the door," called Lucas' anguished voice through their bedroom door.

"Leave me be, Lucas," Nina moaned with her back still pressed against the solid oak. "You should be with Rosalyn. She needs you more than I do at the moment."

With trembling hands, Nina massaged her aching temples. Lucas had conceived a child with Rosalyn, and she, Nina, was pregnant with Stefan's child. It was all such a mess. To Nina, it seemed senseless for her to remain married to Lucas. Nina's heart ached for her unborn child. She did not want her baby to be born into all of this. What kind of mother would she be if she allowed him or her to be brought into this toxic situation? No. Something had to be done...

"I don't want to be with Rosalyn. I want to talk to you, please, Nina," Lucas said.

There was a note of desperation in his voice that Nina had scarcely heard before. Nina knew how relentless Lucas could be, so she wiped away her tears and stood to open the door, taking a deep breath as she took in his features. His blue eyes were wide and bloodshot, and his lower lip was trembling. Nina stood aside to let Lucas pass, and as she closed the door behind him, she steeled herself for the conversation that was to follow.

"I think that we should separate, Luças," Nina said in a voice of feigned bravery.

Lucas faltered for a moment before he took both of Nina's hands in his. "No, no, Nina..." he said, shaking his head as though his words and actions could sway Nina's decision. "I will take care of

Rosalyn's pregnancy. I will stop seeing her, I promise…"

Nina let out a laugh of mingled scorn and amusement. "Come on, Lucas. You have said that you will stop seeing her and all of the others several times over the years. Why not leave me and be with the woman you so obviously desire?"

"Stop it, Nina," Lucas said, shaking his head again and seizing her by the shoulders. When he next spoke, Nina's stomach churned as she realised that he was actually pleading with her.

"I don't want her, I want you! You are my wife; you have given me so much more than she ever could! She is nothing - she is just a fantasy. You are the woman that I truly love!" he cried, gazing imploringly into her eyes.

"It doesn't matter, Lucas," Nina sighed, furiously blinking away more hot tears. "She has a child growing inside of her. Your child. You have a duty to care for her and your baby."

"Nina… please…." Lucas begged, his voice breaking with each word.

Nina felt a twinge of pity for her husband of twenty years. If she did not love Stefan, she might have almost believed Lucas' words and promises. However, experience had taught her to know better.

"When it mattered to me, you refused to stop seeing her and the others," Nina choked. "Now that it has become too real for you, with real consequences, you suddenly change your mind! It is ridiculous. This marriage is over, Lucas." She removed his hands from her shoulders while staring resolutely at the opposite wall to avoid eye contact with him. "I think we both know that it has been over for a long time. You will be happier this way. You can see Rosalyn and do whatever you please. I don't care. And I will be better off not being treated so poorly…"

Lucas' features contorted into a mingled grimace and sneer. Nina backed away from him slowly as her heart beat frantically against her chest. This change in his manner made her feel afraid.

"You can't leave me," he said in a voice barely more than a whisper. "I am your husband and you are my wife. I say no and that is the end of it. I *will* make this work, Nina."

Nina let out a huge sigh of frustration and vehemence. "Lucas, you can't possibly make this work. Rosalyn is pregnant with your child and I… I am pregnant too."

Nina bit her lip as her words hung ominously in the air between them. Lucas began pacing around the room, running his hands through his sleek blond hair.

"How can you be pregnant?" he spat suddenly. "I can't remember the last time that we slept together…"

Nina closed her eyes and wished that she could be anywhere but here. Her insides writhed uncomfortably as she waited for Lucas to put two and two together. She walked over to the bed and sat down, placing her tired head in her hands.

After two uncomfortable minutes, Nina dared to raise her head, looking at Lucas through her fingers. Lucas walked towards her and knelt down at her feet. Nina could feel the anger and rage positively radiating from him. His eyes were narrowed and his teeth were bared.

"You have been unfaithful?" Lucas growled. "Who have you been with? Who has dared to sleep with my wife?"

Nina remained silent and two tears clung to her eyelashes before rolling down her cheeks.

"Answer me, whore! Who have you been sleeping with? Whose bastard child are you carrying?" Lucas roared and raised his hand. Nina winced as he batted her hands away from her face with the back of his hand.

"Nina has been with me," came a calm, quiet voice from behind them. Nina looked up and her heart fluttered at the sight of Stefan framed in the doorway. He looked very calm considering this was the moment that they had never believed would come.

Whatever Lucas was expecting, it was certainly not that.

"Y-you?" Lucas asked, standing up to face Stefan with his eyes wide with shock.

"Yes," Stefan said, looking directly into Lucas' eyes. "Nina is pregnant with my child. We have been together for some time now, and we love each other. Now please do not touch her like that again."

Despite the precariousness of the situation, Nina smiled weakly at Stefan. Her lover, her friend, her soul mate.

"NO!" Lucas roared and lunged forwards at Stefan who side-stepped him and moved closer towards Nina.

Nina could only watch as Lucas paced furiously around the room, knocking things off shelves with his hands. Nina winced as each object crashed to the floor.

"What the fuck, Stefan. You think you can take *my* wife away from me?" Lucas growled again, his knuckles cracking ominously.

"I don't presume to take Nina anywhere. She is a human being with her own mind," Stefan said coolly, running a hand through his sleek, dark hair.

Lucas spat derisively at Stefan's feet. "Don't make me laugh! Jesus, I always knew you were such a pathetic failure in love, but to steal your best friend's wife... that is low, Stefan, even for you."

Stefan smiled. "I don't want to argue with you, Lucas. Nina and I love each other. I know how many times you have been unfaithful to her. Isn't it better for her to be with someone who loves her and treats her properly?"

"I may have strayed, but I always came back!" Lucas yelled, his hands balled tightly into fists. "Nina and I have shared so many special moments and memories - you can't even hope to give her everything that I have given her, Stefan! You know I love you, Nina, don't you?"

He stared at Nina so intently that it made her face burn. After a few excruciating seconds, Nina shook her head despairingly. "No, I know that Stefan loves me, and I love him. I want to be with Stefan."

Lucas began breathing through his nose heavily, too incensed to speak.

Bravely, Stefan broke the tension. "Lucas, it makes sense for you to do the decent thing and support Rosalyn through her pregnancy, as I intend to do with Nina."

"You will not!" Lucas shouted, his anger again bubbling to the surface. He punched the nearby wall with his fist. "No, I will not have this! I will fight you for Nina's love, Stefan!"

"Come now, old friend, stop this foolishness," Stefan said, holding out a steady hand towards Lucas. "Nina's love cannot be won in a fist fight. Let go of your anger. Let us shake hands and sit down as equals to discuss our next steps…"

Let go of his anger? He could as easily sprout a pair of wings, thought Nina.

CHAPTER XXIII

September 1905

The clocks chimed ominously throughout Sinclair manor. The tumultuous storm of emotions had passed, and now Nina was faced with the aftermath. Lucas had attacked Stefan, punching him over and over, and Nina had pleaded with him to stop, almost placing herself in danger. Stefan had not fought back, but had merely assured his friend that he did not want it to come to this, and begged Nina to leave the room so as not to become distressed or hurt. Thankfully, as Stefan had fallen to the ground, William and Lolita, having heard the commotion, had entered the room and intervened, which gave Nina enough time to lift Stefan to his feet and escort him to his room, where she was now caring for him and treating his wounds.

Stefan winced as Nina pressed a cold cloth against his bruised face and mopped up the blood that was seeping from his lower lip.

"Why did you just stand there and let him do that to you?" Nina whispered, choking back tears.

Stefan smiled mournfully and shrugged. "I probably deserved it, Nina. But these bruises and cuts are inconsequential."

Nina pursed her lips. "How so?"

He took her hand in his and raised it to his lips, before speaking again.

"Because they will heal, and now that everyone knows about our relationship, we are free to be together. I couldn't be happier, Nina."

Nina's face broke into a smile. She sincerely hoped that this was the case, but she could not quell the overwhelming suspicion that their relationship was still to be met with more resistance from Lucas and the others. Surely it couldn't be so simple.

Suddenly, the door behind them opened and Nina whirled around in alarm, only to breathe a sigh of relief as she realised that it was Lolita.

"Jesus, Stefan, you look horrific," Lolita said as she walked over to the bed and stood at the opposite side to Nina.

"I appreciate your bedside manner," Stefan said, as Nina glared across the bed at Lolita.

"Where is Lucas?" Nina asked, now applying another cold cloth to the bruises on the other side of Stefan's face.

"Oh, he's with William. I think they have gone out for a drink now." Lolita replied. "He is such a pompous bastard, you know. He has been whining all afternoon - it is pathetic. I nearly had to leave the room, but then I remembered I wanted to relay to you everything that he has said."

"I'm not really interested-" Nina began but Lolita interjected. Despite the seriousness of the situation, Lolita still seemed to revel in the events of the afternoon.

"He was saying how devastated he is that he has been betrayed by you both and then William reminded him that he has been sleeping with other women for years. It was brilliant."

Nina's eyes widened with astonishment. "I thought William would be more annoyed about Stefan and me disrupting the order of *The Shrewd Seven*?"

"Oh, Nina," laughed Lolita. "How can William be concerned with upholding marriages and traditions when he had an affair with me? He doesn't care about any of that anymore. I think my becoming pregnant and having Karina has changed his outlook on things."

Nina and Stefan glanced at each other and let out a collective sigh of relief.

"Anyway, speaking of impregnating people, how come you kept your pregnancy a secret?" Lolita said, smirking and pointing an accusatory finger between Nina and Stefan.

"It was none of your business," Nina said shortly.

"Oh, come on, Nina," laughed Lolita. "I know better than anyone what you are going through. I could have given you my support. Nevertheless, congratulations are in order. I think that you two will make wonderful parents."

Nina's expression softened and Stefan placed his hands on her stomach.

"Thank you, we are very excited," Stefan said and leant up to place a kiss on Nina's cheek.

Nina smiled in spite of herself. "Now Karina will have somebody to play with," she said to her sister.

"That will be lovely," Lolita said.

The two sisters shared a meaningful smile for a moment until Lolita spoke again.

"Well, I would love to stay and chat but alas, William has asked me to convey a message to you, Stefan."

Stefan leaned forwards in the bed and Nina placed her hand on his shoulder.

"As you know, William plans to meet Commissioner Bancroft tomorrow to negotiate the return of our daughter." Lolita began.

Stefan nodded curtly.

"He and Bancroft have agreed that the two of them will meet at the warehouse alone. And William has assured Bancroft that he will return the stolen jewels in exchange for Karina. However, as you may expect, William's true intentions are slightly different..."

Stefan raised his eyebrows. "Of course, go on..."

"William is planning an ambush on Bancroft, and he wants us to accompany him - you, me, Lucas and Daniel. He does not have any of the jewels left to return, and he is furious that Bancroft had the nerve to take our daughter. I think he means to kill him… and for us to assist him with doing so…"

What little colour he had drained from Stefan's face and Nina's stomach plummeted. "Absolutely not!" she said hotly, blinking rapidly. "Stefan is not fit to go anywhere and I don't want any of you to be involved with this. It is too dangerous!"

Lolita shrugged. "It is William's decision, Nina, and this is what he wishes. We need to get our daughter back."

"Yes, but not like this! Have any of you considered the possibility that Bancroft will arrive at the warehouse with an entourage of armed police?" Nina cried, running her hands through her hair.

"Yes, William has thought of this, and it is another reason why he needs us there," Lolita said quietly.

As she glanced at Stefan, Nina noticed that his brow was furrowed. He seemed to be thinking deeply about something.

"Thank you for the message, Lolita," Stefan said at last.

"He wants to meet for debriefing in the morning, can I tell him that you will be there?" Lolita asked.

Stefan nodded.

"Alright, well I will see you tomorrow. And congratulations again," Lolita said and winked, as she walked towards the door and quitted the room.

Now that they were alone, Nina could speak freely with Stefan.

"Stefan, I really do not want you to go to the warehouse tomorrow. It is dangerous. Things might not go the way that William has planned. He cannot predict the actions of the police. Please, Stefan. I don't want any of you to get hurt, or worse…"

Stefan took both of her hands in his and looked deeply into her eyes. "Don't worry, Nina, it won't come to that. I have a plan -

trust me."

CHAPTER XXIV

September 1905

Lolita and Stefan rarely agreed on anything, however they were both adamant that under no circumstances was Nina to accompany them to the old warehouse that night.

"What am I supposed to do here by myself while everyone I love is out there doing God knows what?" Nina had cried in earnest. Stefan had shook his head and held her in his arms, placing a gentle kiss on her forehead. He told her not to worry, that they would be back soon and that if she was to go there with them it would cause unnecessary stress for her and their unborn baby. Nina had protested all afternoon and she had almost been sick with worry as she had watched them drive away.

She did not know how long ago they had left, but it must have been a few hours at least, as the sky had darkened and the outside oil lamps had been lit. To distract herself, Nina had been painting at her easel in the drawing room of Sinclair Manor as this was the only thing that she could do which would require her full attention.

The stars were twinkling in the dark sky outside and the moonlight streamed in through the window, bathing the room in a silvery glow. Nina tore her eyes away from her half-finished painting of a mountain and a sunset, and drew the curtains closed. She lit the oil lamps in the room and tossed the match into the fireplace with a view to start the fire as the room was becoming chilly. As the oil lamps flickered and the fire started crackling in its grate, once again Nina lifted her paintbrush. With precision, she dipped the tip of the brush into the deep scarlet paint and swirled it around. Just as she was about to put her brush back to the canvas to resume painting the red sky around the sunset, the drawing room doors burst open and Nina's maid Lottie ran into the room with wide, frantic eyes and a pale face.

"Mistress Nina!" Lottie cried.

Nina was so startled that she dropped her paintbrush and palette. As they clattered to the ground, flecks of scarlet paint flew everywhere, staining the canvas, the easel, the carpet, and the curtains.

"What is it, Lottie?" Nina asked, stooping to try and mop up some of the paint.

"Leave the paint, I will clean it later," Lottie continued breathlessly. "Some of the servants have been in London tonight and they say there is a commotion at the old warehouse where Master Lucas and the others have been!"

Nina's stomach lurched. "What kind of commotion?"

"They say there are police cars and ambulances everywhere, and-" The young girl faltered, gulping and taking a deep breath. "They say two people have been shot and taken to hospital."

Tears welled up behind Nina's eyes. Her heart started beating rapidly and she could hear the blood pumping in her ears.

"Prepare a carriage for me at once," Nina said in a hollow sort of voice and with trembling hands she reached for her coat from the nearby coat stand.

"Of course," Lottie said and immediately left the room.

*

An emotion quite unlike anything Nina had ever experienced was surging through her body like wildfire as she strode through the hospital doors with only one thing on her mind. Her lungs felt as though they were shrivelling, her breath was hitched in her throat and she knew that it would remain so until she knew for certain what had happened.

She couldn't breathe, she couldn't think, she could only see the white-washed walls and hear the clattering of her heeled boots on the cold, hard, hospital floor as she ran towards the accident and emergency department. Everything else in the world was, at this moment, irrelevant. She needed to know who had been injured and what their condition was.

"Where are the casualties from the warehouse?" Nina asked the nurse behind the desk when she arrived at last. Her voice was as calm as she could possibly make it, given the frantic thoughts racing around her mind. She looked around the room. The hospital waiting area was filled with people bustling around. The nurse considered Nina for a moment before replying. She looked as though she were on the verge of saying something of vital importance.

"Are you a family member?" The nurse said, looking at her clipboard, and surveying Nina with an ambiguous expression.

"I - yes - well I don't know. It depends-" Nina began, but as she spoke, Lucas suddenly emerged from a door to the right of the desk. His face was very pale and as his eyes fell on Nina, he wiped the sweat from his forehead with shaking hands.

"Lucas!" Nina cried and rushed over to him. He opened his arms and embraced her. She buried her head in his chest. It was almost as though the last few days had not happened; that he had not found out about her affair with Stefan, that everything was as it used to be between them...

"What has happened?" She wailed. "Who has been hurt?"

As they slowly broke apart, Lucas gazed deeply into her eyes. His lips trembled as he next spoke. "Stefan and William have both been shot. They are in surgery now. We are not allowed in."

Panic soared through Nina's veins, her stomach constricted and her heart panged with sorrow.

"What? Is Stefan okay? Is he going to be alright?" She said, wringing her hands and beginning to cry.

Before Lucas could reply, Daniel and Lolita appeared in the doorway - Lolita had clearly retrieved baby Karina and was holding on to her daughter as though she would never let her go again. Daniel had a frightened expression on his face and Lolita looked like a shell of her former self. Usually so full of words and emotion, she now looked broken. She was pale and clammy; her cheeks were tear-stained and her eye makeup was smudged and smeared.

"Oh thank goodness you are alright, Danny," Nina said, walking over to him and kissing him, her tears seeping onto his cheeks. "And you, Lolita. I have been so worried about you all. And thank heavens Karina is safe…"

Lolita did not speak. Her eyes were fixed resolutely on the floor and her lips were pursed as she rocked her crying daughter.

Nina felt so overwhelmed with all of the emotions surging through her body. A wave of nausea fell over her and her legs began to buckle beneath her. Fortunately, Daniel caught her before her knees hit the ground. Together, Daniel and Lucas escorted Nina to a nearby seat and they all sat together in the waiting area.

"Is Stefan going to be alright?" Nina repeated, taking a deep breath to steady herself.

Lucas and Daniel exchanged glances. Lolita said nothing but held baby Karina close to her.

"It is hard to say, Nina. We just need to wait and let the doctors do their best for him now." Lucas said quietly. He obviously didn't say what he was really thinking because the look on his face was frightening for Nina. She gulped.

"Can somebody please tell me what happened?" She cried, digging her fingernails into her cheeks in frustration.

There was a pause.

"Stefan is stupid and that peeler is a sly bastard," Lolita said at last in a cold voice. "That's what happened. And now who knows if William and Stefan are going to survive? My girl might have to grow up without a father because Stefan had a sudden attack of conscience." Lolita spat bitterly on the floor and stood up. She gave them all a cold, withering look, turned on her heel and swept out of the room, leaving a shocked and uncomfortable silence in her wake.

Nina was the first to break it. With tears rolling down her cheeks and her hands balled into fists she began to shout. "What does she mean? Lucas, Daniel, please tell me what happened? I need to know!"

Lucas and Daniel exchanged glances once again. Daniel nodded his head at his father and Lucas closed his eyes and wiped his brow.

"It is a long story, Nina," He began. "Are you sure you want me to tell you, given your... condition?" He winced as he said the words.

"Of course, I need to know!" Nina said again.

"Alright," Lucas began wearily. "We arrived at the old warehouse earlier this evening. As William suspected, Bancroft had brought some other policemen with him. Bancroft and William hurled a few insults at each other. Next thing, Stefan revealed that he had retrieved all of the jewels that William sold and he gave them to Bancroft. We were all obviously surprised as that wasn't part of William's plan. Stefan begged Bancroft to put all this business behind him, to return the child and let us all go on our way..."

Nina was stunned. Stefan had done the sensible thing after all. Despite her panic and trepidation, her heart swelled with pride. "Go on," She said, prompting Lucas to continue.

"It wasn't to be so simple. William was furious. He said that their feud wasn't even about the jewels now. He said that because Bancroft had kidnapped their baby daughter that this had become a personal matter. There was a fist fight between Bancroft and William. They exchanged a few punches and we tried to break it up. Then, William took out his gun and shot at Bancroft, but for some reason, Stefan threw himself in front of him and took the hit, saving Bancroft's life."

Nina gasped. "Oh my God!" She put her head in her hands.

"William was obviously shocked when Stefan fell to the ground," Lucas continued darkly. "So Bancroft took advantage of his lapse in attention and shot William in the stomach."

Nina let out a huge moan with her head still in her hands. Daniel put his arms around his mother and comforted her as she sobbed.

"So then Bancroft left to call the ambulance and they took William and Stefan away, bringing them here. One of Bancroft's men gave baby Karina back to Lolita and then we all rushed here. We stayed with William and Stefan until the doctors took them into surgery. And now here we are with you." Lucas finished the story and his voice began to break with emotion. "I wish there was more I could have done to help, but it just all happened so fast. None of us could have predicted what happened."

CHAPTER XXV

September 1905

Most of the night had now passed. The hours had ticked by so slowly that it was excruciating. The clock on the waiting room wall ticked loudly as though it was mocking them. Most of the other patients and visitors had now left the hospital. William was out of theatre and was recovering in a hospital bed in a private room. Lolita had returned and had disappeared to be with William as soon as she was able to.

Lucas and Daniel, however, had stayed with Nina. There was still no news of Stefan and by now, Nina was fearing the worst. She was feeling incredibly nauseous and kept pacing around the room. She knew that this stress would not be good for her unborn baby but it could not be helped, given the situation. She caressed her stomach surreptitiously, muttering "Your father will be okay, baby," under her breath, as if to comfort the baby, when in all honesty it was to comfort herself.

All of a sudden, the double doors to the waiting room swung open at last, and a doctor emerged, removing his glasses and stethoscope. Nina darted over to the door.

"How is Stefan?" She asked in desperation, twisting her hands together. Lucas and Daniel also stood and came over to join Nina and the doctor.

The doctor bestowed Nina with a sorrowful gaze. "I - I think you had better sit down, m'am."

Those dreaded words.

Nina didn't need to hear what he had to say, for it was written all over his face.

"No - no - no - don't look at me like that, please." Nina said, tears once again welling up behind her eyes. Her chin quivered and her legs trembled as she sat down on her seat again.

The doctor sat down beside her. Words failed Nina as he took a deep breath. Lucas took hold of Nina's hand in his and gave it a squeeze. Nina could no longer speak; she was overwhelmed with fear and dawning comprehension, and put her hand to her heart. She savoured the moments before the doctor spoke again. If he didn't speak then it couldn't be true…

"I am a colleague of Stefan's here at the hospital," the doctor began. "As you know, Stefan was badly injured. He sustained a gunshot wound to the abdomen. We tried our best to remove the bullet and to help him through this, however, he lost a lot of blood, and I am sorry to say that Stefan passed away a few moments ago."

As those last few words drifted through Nina's ears and connected semantically with her mind, a stabbing pain coursed through her chest and it felt as though her heart had shattered. The world seemed to invert itself and come to a stand-still. She became aware of Lucas taking her into his arms, but after this, Nina couldn't really remember what happened next, other than feeling as though she was falling into a bottomless black hole of despair. Her whole body had turned to ice. She was so overcome with shock that the news did not sink in for some time, or maybe she refused to accept it. Through her haze of pain and suffering, she peered again at the doctor. He was still gazing at her sympathetically. Nina tried to speak but no words came out.

"I can only offer you all my deepest condolences," the doctor said. "Stefan was a great man. It was an honour to have worked alongside him here."

To Nina, the words seemed to come from very far away. She nodded, suddenly becoming aware that her head was resting on Lucas' chest. She was staring at the doctor but not really seeing him. Tears froze like icicles, balancing precariously on the lids of her eyes.

"Was he in pain?" Nina croaked so feebly that she must have been incoherent.

"I'm sorry?"

"Was he in pain," she asked, a little more clearly, "when he died?"

"I wouldn't have thought so," said the doctor. "We had given him lots of pain relief. They say that before you die it is quite peaceful, you know."

Nina mumbled words of thanks, trying to quell sudden and vivid mental images of Stefan's last living moments. The doctor walked away and Nina began to cry harder than she had ever cried in her life. Daniel sat with his head in his hands. Lucas held Nina tightly as she sobbed and sobbed. He did not speak although she could feel his own tears dripping down onto her cheek, as her head was resting on his shoulder.

It was over. Stefan was gone. The man she loved would never again hold her, kiss her, talk to her, or smile at her. Their dreams of their new life together were shattered along with Nina's heart. Her unborn baby would never know her father…

Nina did not know how long she sat there crying in Lucas' arms. Her whole world had come crashing down around her and all she could do was sit there as frozen as an ice sculpture and as devastated as a shipwreck in a stormy sea.

*

The next few days passed by in a blur to Nina. She had returned to Sinclair Manor and had spent all her time in Stefan's bedroom, lying in his bed or else sitting on the settee thinking about him and all of the special times they had shared together in that very room and elsewhere. Apparently Stefan had written a letter to Nina shortly before he went into theatre and one of the doctors from the hospital had delivered it to Nina earlier that morning.

As of yet, she did not have the strength or the courage to read it, because seeing his words on the parchment, and knowing that his hand had glided over it shortly before he died was too painful for her.

Lucas and Daniel had also returned to the Manor and had been caring for Nina, bringing her food and water and helping her to bathe and dress, as she had become so withdrawn into herself that she couldn't even look after herself properly. Lolita, however, was still at the hospital, sitting dutifully at William's bedside, willing him to return to perfect health. According to Lucas, William's health was slowly starting to decline again but Lolita was determined that he would make a full recovery. Lucas had suggested that they bring Karina back to the Manor as he felt that she would be better away from her father's bedside but Lolita had refused to hand her over, stating that she was not letting the child out of her sight.

The grandfather clock in Stefan's bedroom chimed three times, breaking Nina out of her reverie. Her eyes fell again onto the envelope that was sitting on the coffee table. Stefan had written her name on the front of the envelope in his elegant, cursive handwriting. Although her heart ached at the thought of reading the letter, curiosity suddenly got the better of Nina and she reached for the knife lying next to it in order to cut the envelope open.

As she unfolded the parchment within with trembling hands, tears began to fall from her weary eyes once again. As she read Stefan's words, she imagined his voice and lamented that she would never hear it again.

My darling Nina, if you are reading this then I must have passed away. I told the doctors that if I survive the surgery they are to destroy this letter but if I die they are to give it to you.

My beautiful Nina, I am so sorry to have caused you this pain. I hope that I will recover and we can put this awful ordeal behind us. I was so looking forward to marrying you and having this baby with you, but I really fear that this is not meant to be, Nina. I know the extent of my injuries and I think they may prove fatal. I'm sorry, Nina. I love you so much and I don't want to leave you.

My heart aches at the thought of not seeing you again. Yes, if it happens, my death will be painful, but I want you to know that I will always be with you in your heart. I want to reassure you that you and our baby will be okay. You are a fighter, Nina, I believe that you will get through this and that you will raise our baby with enough love for the both of us.

I never would have dreamed that things would turn out like this, but I think it is important for me to tell you why I took the bullet that was meant for Bancroft.

James Bancroft is the biological son of my late wife, Lara. She gave birth to him and gave him up for adoption long before I met her. She was a young, unmarried girl when she had him, and could not provide for him. On her deathbed, Lara told me of this, and made me promise that I would look out for her son. And so I have done, in secret, all these years. James himself does not even know about it. I knew that he had joined the police and it was my greatest fear that we, the Seven, would have dealings with him because I knew that my loyalty to Lara and my promise to her would have to come before my loyalty to the Seven.

I tried my best to avoid this, Nina. I retrieved the stolen jewels and gave them to James in the hope that all of the animosity between the Seven and the police would be over. I did not think that William would behave as he did. When he pulled the gun on James I had no choice but to honour my promise to Lara. I could not let Lara's son take the bullet if there was a chance that I could stop it. I hope that you understand this, Nina, even if it means that I lose my life. I really did think that once I gave James the jewels that would be the end of it all, but alas, it wasn't to play out as I had hoped. I had intended to tell you of this upon my return to the manor, and I am now sorry that I did not tell you beforehand. Please forgive me, Nina.

I have one thing to ask of you, Nina. If I die, please take this letter to

James and explain it all to him. I hope very much that if nothing else, my returning of the jewels and taking the bullet for him will end his feud with the Seven and that all of the members of the Shrewd Seven can go free.

I love you, Nina. Stay strong. I will try to do the same.

All my love, always,

Stefan

As Nina finished reading the letter, her eyes stung and she bit her lip to stop her tears from falling again. She must have sat there for over an hour, mulling it all over, and visualising the events of that awful night over and over. She wondered how on earth Stefan had even had the strength to write the letter to her. It must have taken all of his might in his last waking moments. A small part of her was hurt that Stefan had not previously told her about his connection to Bancroft but mostly, she felt a sense of pride that Stefan was such an honourable man who kept his promises and risked his own health and safety for the greater good. In the back of her mind, she wished, selfishly, that Bancroft had died and Stefan had lived. However, she had to remind herself that wasn't what Stefan would have wanted, after all.

All of a sudden, she resolved to do what Stefan asked and tell Bancroft about the letter. She steeled herself for her trip to the police station, and hoped that Bancroft would respond favourably to this news about his biological mother. However, getting to the front door of Sinclair Manor without alerting Lucas and Daniel was probably going to be more challenging than speaking with the Commissioner…

CHAPTER XXVI

September 1905

James Bancroft's office at the police station was small, dark, and windowless. The walls were adorned with various photographs and newspaper clippings that related to the many crimes that the police force were currently investigating. Bancroft's desk was cluttered with stacks of paper and books, and there was a wooden case perched upon the desk which contained various medals commemorating his many policing achievements. Becoming Police Commissioner at such a young age seemed extraordinary to Nina. He was obviously very good at his job and Stefan had probably been extremely proud of Bancroft's successes.

Bancroft had been more than surprised when Nina had entered the station and had introduced herself. He had been very polite and charming, offering her a cup of tea and expressing his condolences for Stefan's passing. He was later suitably confused when Nina had handed him the letter that Stefan had written.

Bancroft's brow became more and more furrowed the longer his eyes devoured the piece of parchment. Nina watched him intently as he read the letter, and she had to admit that he was a very handsome young man with his round blue eyes, his sleek fair hair and his well-groomed facial hair. At long last, Bancroft let out a long, low sigh and his hardened facial expression softened.

"Did you love Stefan?" He asked quietly, resting his head on his hands and regarding her over his interlocked fingers.

"Very much," Nina replied.

"And you are carrying his child?"

"Yes," Nina said, choking back tears.

Bancroft handed her a handkerchief and shook his head.

"I cannot believe this," he murmured, tracing his bottom lip with his finger. "I never knew that my mother had been married."

"No, nobody did," Nina explained. "Stefan and your mother were married in secret."

"It does, however, make a lot of sense now," Bancroft continued. "My adoptive parents told me that there was a benefactor who left a great deal of money for me. I never knew who it was, but now I suppose that it was Stefan all along…"

Nina dabbed at her eyes with the handkerchief.

"Yes, I suppose that it was," she said as more tears clung to her eyelashes.

Bancroft sighed deeply.

"Stefan saved my life, and that is something that I will never be able to thank him for now," Bancroft began. "I wish I had known that he had been my benefactor - I won't be able to thank him for that either. However, the longer I consider this, the more I think that I owe it to him to support his unborn child in any way that I can."

Nina nodded. She was incredibly touched by this, but before she could speak, she became distinctly aware of a commotion outside of the room.

Bancroft frowned and stood up, but before he reached the door of his office, it opened with a bang to reveal two police officers restraining an irate brunette woman who was shouting and crying. Nina sighed as she realised that it was, of course, Lolita. There was a third police officer standing behind them holding baby Karina. Lolita was struggling against the officers but she was unable to break free of their grip on her arms. Her eyes were popping wildly, her eye makeup was smudged, and her teeth were bared, giving her a rather frightening appearance.

"Commissioner Bancroft, we have apprehended -" One of the officers began, but Lolita cut across him.

"Bancroft, you piece of shit!" She spat. "Are you happy now that my William is dead?"

Her words sharply pierced the already oppressive atmosphere of the office.

"What? When did this happen?" Bancroft asked.

"Just now, I watched him die in the hospital!" Lolita shrieked, angry tears spilling from her eyes. "So thanks to you, I have lost my lover and my poor daughter has lost her father! I suppose that is what you wanted, to ruin my life? To ruin my daughter's life? Are you happy now?"

"Not exactly, Lolita, but shooting William was the only way to stop him," Bancroft said slowly, walking over to her and standing just out of her reach.

Lolita spat at him, narrowly missing his face.

"Don't lie, you had it in for William! Tell your men to unhand me and face me yourself, you coward!"

Bancroft took a few breaths to steady himself. He looked angry but when he spoke again, his voice was very measured and calm.

"Lolita, it was never my intention to kill William. Might I remind you that he fired the first shot? I merely intended to defend myself and to bring William to justice. I hoped to debilitate and eventually arrest him. It is unfortunate that he has died, as I would have preferred for him to serve life in prison, but I do not regret shooting him. William was a dangerous man and London will be better off without him. I think in time, you will see this, Lolita."

"Like hell!" Lolita cried. "I hate you for what you have done! I will never forgive you and I will never forget this!"

A pained expression crossed Bancroft's face for a fraction of a second. Nina thought for a moment that despite everything, Bancroft might have harboured feelings for and cared for Lolita in some capacity. They had spent the night together all those months ago, after all.

As Bancroft and Lolita continued to argue, a wave of relief swept over Nina, and she closed her eyes as she became immersed in her own thoughts. William was dead. His tyranny had finally come to an end. What would this mean for the *Shrewd Seven*? She felt for her sister and her niece of course, but she had to agree with Bancroft that William's death would probably be a blessing in disguise. Nina opened her eyes again and looked at her sister's face which was now shining with fresh tears.

"I will not apologise for stopping a dangerous criminal," Bancroft said quietly, and took a step towards Lolita as though to try and comfort her.

"Perhaps it is you who is dangerous!" Lolita shouted again. "What kind of monster kidnaps a baby?"

Bancroft closed his eyes and gulped.

"I apologise for taking your baby, but it was the only thing that William would respond to - I had to put an end to his criminality. He was unstoppable. As a policeman, sometimes you have to do things that you are uncomfortable with in order to ensure that the proper person is brought to justice. Your baby was never in any danger - we looked after her, and we knew that by taking her, we would be able to bring William to us. I think it would be best if we continued this discussion once you have calmed down, Lolita."

"How can I calm down?" Lolita shouted, beginning to cry again in earnest. "William is gone! You killed him! I am going to kill you for this, you sly bastard!"

Bancroft shook his head despondently and addressed the officers restraining Lolita.

"Take her into custody for tonight, and I will talk to her tomorrow morning."

"Very good, Sir." One of the officers said, and with that, they clapped handcuffs on Lolita's wrists and escorted her out of the room. The third officer holding Karina stepped forward.

"What about the baby, Sir?"

"Nina, can you look after the baby for tonight?" Bancroft asked.

"Of course," Nina said, taking the child from the police officer, who then left the room to help the other officers.

"I am so sorry for my sister's behaviour," Nina said to Bancroft as she rocked Karina gently in her arms.

"You don't need to apologise for her," Bancroft said, smiling at her. "I understand her anger. She obviously loved William very much. I hope that in time she realises that you will all be much better off without him."

"I do hope that is true," Nina agreed.

Bancroft sat down at his desk again, and put his head in his hands. Nina stayed silent and stroked Karina's face as she fell asleep. After a few moments of deep thought, Bancroft spoke again.

"Now that William is gone, and knowing that Stefan gave his life for mine, I think it is only reasonable that I cease my investigation into *The Shrewd Seven*."

'Oh, really, would you?" Nina said, reaching one hand across the desk and taking his hand in hers.

"On one condition, however," Bancroft continued. "*The Shrewd Seven* must rebrand itself and renounce all criminal activity. It must operate as a legal business, otherwise I will have no choice but to reopen the investigation and uphold my values as Police Commissioner."

Nina nodded. "Of course. I will relay this message to all of the men upon my return home."

Nina stood to leave, and as she started to walk away, Bancroft called after her.

"I meant what I said, I will do my best to support your unborn child. And Lolita's child, if she allows me to. It is, after all, probably my fault that both of your babies no longer have fathers..."

Nina smiled, thanked Bancroft and left the room, before her eyes could deceive her by crying again. She was determined to tell Lucas and the other men all about the events of the evening, and hoped very much that she would be able to put all of this *Shrewd Seven* business behind her.

CHAPTER XXVII

March 1906

After Nina had told Lucas about her meeting with Bancroft, he had held an urgent meeting with all of the remaining *Shrewd Seven* members. During this meeting, it had been decided that Lucas would replace William as the head of the *Seven* and that they would use the money the society had amassed over the years to open a chain of public houses, therefore investing and earning their money by legal means.

Due to the fact that they were no longer on the police's watchlist, the other members of the *Seven* had moved back into their own homes. Nina was now nearing the end of her pregnancy, and she had been living alone and grieving in Sinclair Manor, after having insisted that Lucas and Daniel move back into Monroe Manor. Lucas had initially protested and had asked Nina to move back with them, but Nina reminded him that had Stefan been alive, she would have left Lucas to live with him. Though initially angry and upset, Lucas had accepted this and had resigned himself to the fact that he was to live separate from his wife. He did, however, visit Sinclair Manor to care for Nina throughout her pregnancy. During one of these visits, Lucas had told Nina that Rosalyn Whittaker had miscarried her baby and that he had ended his relationship with her for good, stating that being with her was a mistake and he would regret being unfaithful to Nina for the rest of his life. Lucas had also repeatedly told Nina that he intended to earn back her love, no matter how long it would take. Nina was in no position to refuse his offer of help as there was nobody else that she could turn to and she had been quite ill during the pregnancy, although she doubted that she could ever rekindle her relationship with Lucas.

Her relationship with Lolita was also strained, at best, owing to the fact that Lolita blamed Stefan for William's death. "If it wasn't for your stupid lover, I wouldn't be in this mess! If Stefan didn't take the bullet, Bancroft would be dead and William would still be alive!" Lolita had cried during their last argument, after Lolita had spent the night in a prison cell at Bancroft's behest. The two sisters had not spoken since this, as Lolita was extremely stubborn, so Nina did not really know how her sister was coping with William's death. All she had to go on was Lucas' accounts that Lolita was keeping herself busy with the *Seven*'s new business ventures, and that Bancroft had been attempting to send reams of cash to Lolita in order to provide support for Karina, which she had been shredding in temper before returning to him.

It was so hard to believe that it had been six months since Stefan's and William's deaths. On one sunny Spring morning, Nina was sitting on a settee in the drawing room of Sinclair Manor, reading a book of John Donne's poetry, when there was a knock at the front door. Nina groaned. She did not have the strength nor the energy to greet any visitors owing to the size of her ever-growing midsection. She supposed that one of the servants had answered the door as she heard voices in the hallway and footsteps approaching the drawing room. As the door opened, Nina's eyes became wide as she beheld none other than Lolita standing before her with her hands on her hips.

"Jesus, look at you," Lolita said. "You look like you're ready to burst."

"How lovely to see you too, sister," Nina said coldly. "To what do I owe the pleasure of your visit after all this time?"

"Oh, stop with that tone, Nina," Lolita said, waving a hand dismissively and rolling her eyes. "There is somebody here that I thought you would like to see again."

"Oh?" Nina asked, raising herself into more of an upright seated position.

Lolita beckoned to someone on the other side of the door, and to Nina's utter astonishment, their sister Evangeline stepped into the room. Although Evangeline's features were somewhat softer, her makeup more natural, and her hair and eyes a lighter brown, she still resembled Lolita more closely than Nina did. Evangeline was wearing a plain, beige coloured dress and she seemed more frail than the last time that Nina had seen her. There was a lingering sadness behind her eyes which told Nina that the past year had been tough for her.

"Hello Nina," Evangeline said, smiling weakly. "I believe that we have a lot of catching up to do."

With tremendous effort, Nina stood and walked over to hug Evangeline. She sobbed into her sister's shoulder for a few moments before motioning for her to sit down on the settee next to her. Lolita summoned a servant to get them some drinks before joining them on the settee, and the three sisters spent a long time getting reacquainted with each other.

Apparently, Evangeline and her daughter Myrcella had heard that William had died so they had deemed it safe to return to their old house. Evangeline spoke at length about how painful her husband Thomas' death had been, and the toll it had taken on her health, but she hoped that now she had returned to be with family, her health and well-being would improve. Nina updated Evangeline on everything that had transpired during her absence - her affair with Stefan, her pregnancy, the events at the warehouse, how Lucas was hoping to win back her affections, Stefan's letter, her last argument with Lolita - all of it.

Evangeline listened intently. When Nina had finished, Evangeline told her that she should consider giving Lucas one last chance as he clearly loved her. She explained that Nina shouldn't take this love for granted, and suggested that she and Lucas could raise Stefan's child together. Nina was unsure about this, but she supposed that her sister meant well and was talking as someone who had lost her husband. Evangeline then insisted that Nina and Lolita make amends. She made them hug like they did when they were girls after falling out, and said that life was too short to be angry with one's family members. Although hesitant and resolute at first, Nina and Lolita eventually agreed and they both began to cry as they hugged, each apologising for not being there to support the other through their grief. They accepted that they couldn't change what had taken place between the men on that awful night, and that they may as well try and move forward as friends, as now of course they had their babies to think of as well as themselves.

As Nina and Lolita broke apart from their embrace, Nina felt a peculiar sensation in her lower abdomen that she had only ever felt once before. Sure enough, pain seared through her body and she leant forward, clutching her stomach and breathing quickly.

"Oh my God, Nina! Are you alright?" Evangeline cried.

"What is it?" Lolita said in alarm.

"I think - I think my baby is coming!" Nina said breathlessly.

Evangeline opened her mouth in shock.

"How wonderful!" She cried, and jumped up to call for the servants to bring them some towels and bedsheets.

For Nina, panic was setting in. Until this moment, she had forgotten what the pain of labour was like, but now that it was starting again, it all came flooding back to her and she suddenly remembered it all too well. She had last given birth over seventeen years ago, and had been much younger and fitter then. What if it was more difficult and more painful this time?

"Will you stay with me?" Nina asked Lolita, squeezing her hand.

"Of course, Nina," Lolita said. "You helped to deliver Karina and so it is my turn to help you. Don't worry, everything is going to be alright - we are here with you."

EPILOGUE

March 1910

Dearest Stefan,

It has been four years since you passed and here I am writing to you as though nothing has changed; as though we are still writing secret letters in the Shakespeare book. My new physician believes that it will help with my grief if I write a letter to you as though you were alive. I am willing to try this, as not a day goes by where I don't miss you and where I don't think of all of the special times we shared together.

I would like to start by telling you that we have a beautiful four-year-old daughter, Juliet Stephanie Belle Sinclair. She has your dark hair, my blue eyes and she definitely has inherited your intelligence. She is such a clever little girl, and just yesterday she told me that she wants to be a nurse at the hospital when she grows up! I have told her all about you, of course, and how wonderful you were. I have also shown photographs of you to her and she says she is proud that she looks like you!

I lived at Sinclair Manor for a while after your passing, but shortly after giving birth to Juliet I moved back to Monroe Manor with Lucas. Your brother Harry is currently living at your old house but he assures me that it will go to Juliet once she becomes of age.

I hope you would not be upset with me for reconciling with Lucas, but he has been very loyal and kind to me, and has been a tremendous help with Juliet. He is so good with her, and has helped me to raise her as if she was his own. He said that he has done this to honour you, as despite everything, you were always his best friend. He knows that I would have left him for you had you still been alive. I will never love him again in the way that I love you, Stefan - it is a different kind of love that I have for him, I think. I don't think our marriage will ever return to what it was in the beginning, but it works for us at the moment.

Lolita and Karina are living here with us at Monroe Manor. It is nice for the girls as they share the same governess and they get to spend all of their time together, but it is also nice for Lolita and me to have each other's company, as we did not speak for a while after your death.

Karina has also turned into a beautiful little girl, and she and Juliet are great friends. She looks just like Lolita and thankfully she does not seem to have inherited any of her father's cruelness. James Bancroft has made good on his promise to support our children and has been sending money for both Juliet and Karina, which I think is so honourable of him. He says that he sees it as his way of thanking you for being his own benefactor all those years ago, and his way of honouring your sacrifice. He and Lolita seem to be getting along better these days, too; he has recently proposed marriage to her, but you know Lolita - she is keeping him at arm's length for now. I do hope she sees sense! Could you imagine William's face if he could see Lolita marrying Bancroft? And Bancroft bringing up his daughter? It doesn't bear thinking about, does it? Karina even said the other day that she wants to be a policewoman in the future; I think William would turn in his grave if he knew!

I also wish you could see all of the positive changes that have happened within The Shrewd Seven. *Lucas has made it into a very successful legal business now. They have opened pubs, restaurants and hotels in London which have all been doing very well, and there is even talk of them opening more in other cities! How I wish you could have been a part of this, Stefan!*

Things are also going very well at the hospital. Daniel has completed all of his training and he is a qualified doctor, working in your old department. I am so proud of him and I hope that you would be, too! He and Anita have married and they have a baby on the way. I cannot believe that I will soon be a grandmother, but I am so excited to meet the little one.

I want to reassure you that Juliet and I are okay. We miss you and we love you, of course, but I have tried my best to bring her up with as much love as possible. It has been so incredibly difficult at times, because I wish we were raising her together, but I understand that I can't change this and that I just have to put her needs before my own.

I hope very much that you are in a better place with no pain or suffering, and that you are watching over us. I hope that I live the rest of my life making you proud. I will always love you and I will never forget you. I long for a time when I can look into your eyes and see you looking back at me again. Goodbye for now, Stefan. Until we meet again in Heaven.

Yours, always, Nina

THE END

Printed in Great Britain
by Amazon